SNOWDROPS

FROM A

CURATE'S GARDEN

1881 A. D.

COSMOPOLI

IMPRIMÉ SOUS LE MANTEAU
ET NE SE VEND
NULLE PART

BIRCHGROVE PRESS

http://www.birchgrovepress.com

ISBN:
978-0-9870956-4-0

A riotous parody of pornographic writing in prose and verse, *Snowdrops from a Curate's Garden* was first published clandestinely in France c. 1904. It was written by the influential libertine-mystic and magician, Aleister Crowley (1875-1947), primarily to amuse his convalescing wife, Rose Kelly, and published privately. It was most probably printed by Phillipe Renouard in Paris.

SNOWDROPS

FROM A

CURATE'S GARDEN

CONTENTS

JUVENILIA

THE BROMO BOOK

PARODIES

LIMERICKS

INTRODUCTION

Two philosophers of an empirical type, R. Browning and J. Christ, agree in disputing the possibility of obtaining a silk purse from the traditional sow's ear. Can rapes spring from horns? Or pigs from whistles? asks the latter; while the former (by the mouth of his sophistical hero Caponsacchi), declines to believe the sexton who claims to have transfixed a scorpion in the very act of issuing from the mouth of Madonna, and suggests (what seems to us quite as improbable) that it issued from the sexton himself...

> "Like from like,
> By way o the ordure corner..."

At first sight it may seem that Science endorses this dogma in its fullest sense; but the truth is that if we apply the fundamental fact to man, we are led into error. For the nature of no man is simple thorn or simple grape: in the incalculable tale of his ancestors must inevitably be found, not only both these types, but a host of others.

Further, in the complex chemical nature of the cerebral secretions lies the profound possibility of extraordinary divergence from the normal. So many, so fickle, are the combinations which constitute Cerebrin, Lethicin, and the rest; so subtly is the thought dependent upon changes proximate or remote in the composition of the organism, that we must expect character — which is but the statement of the sum of deep-seated habits of thought — to show similar instability. The word habit may seem to invalidate such a conclusion; but must we expect habits to be homogenous? Must the religious man be also merciful? We know that it is not so.

In the infinite variety of character thus formed we occasionally meet a case in which distaste of the normal, vital scepticism, or some similar trait, may push the individual to contrary poles of thought and action. We shall err if we fail to recognise the common basis of the audacities of piety and impiety which may manifest in the same man.

As one of our great specialists has shewn, it is unphilosophical, indeed contrary to proved fact, to suppose that a man like Jabez Balfour is necessarily insincere. His cruel frauds, his callous scepticism are no less genuine and no more so than his narrow religious convictions. As well accuse a typewriter of deceit because it is capable of writing both the brilliant good sense of a Hall Caine and the vapourish outpourings of a Meredith!

As well accuse a spaniel of hypocrisy because he will retrieve game, and yet refuse to devour it.

The outlines of this truth have been allegorically sketched by R. L. Stevenson in "Dr. Jekyll and Mr. Hyde." Outlines, for in reality there are as many sides to character as there are ideas capable of influencing the individual. No doubt, in all cases the one is leavened by the many; even in stark madness there is an underlying essential harmony. This is of course the case, but such harmony dwells far deeper than anything which we commonly intend by character.

Such an expression of violences is found in the author of the following works.

It is the custom to study, even if briefly, the life of a great writer from the biographical standpoint. In this case it is impossible to follow the usual course, for I have no wish to blast the useful public career of the most talented artist of our day, and there can be no doubt that precision of allusion would cause his innumerable friends to recognize in the infamous blackguard who penned these abominations the saintly and delicate-minded hero of their dreams.

But there is at my disposal sufficient matter of a noncommittal character to enable me to indicate for the purposes of the student the circumstances in which K. has lived, and lives. He was born about the year 1860 in a hunting shire of England. His parents were of that lesser class of county magnate which does not care to make any great show. They had enough self-respect to live the life of their choice. The boy, delicate in his youth, was not able to bear the roughness of public school for long, but he passed with honours through Oxford, respected for his piety and learning by his professors and (I am ashamed to say) adored by a certain unsavoury coterie for the babyish beauty of his face, with its unfathomable eyes, its small and scarlet mouth, and the impudent cynicism of his — bottomless lust, I would say, but for the peculiar inappropriateness of the epithet. In a word he was the foremost scholar and courtesan of his year.

It would be admittedly ridiculous to claim the latter note of his life as hypocritical; only prigs will so stigmatize the former. A boy of 20 does not render Thomas à Kempis into Greek Anapaests without genuine scholarship and equally sincere piety. Yet he is the author of the nauseous hexameters beginning:

"Hail to the f...ting lips of an open Athenian a...."

He it was who capped the hexameter in St. James:

"Husbands! Love your wives and be not bitter against them!" with

"Husbands! F... them often, or surely somebody else will!"

A few examples of his quaint, often recondite, wit will delight all who hear.

One night in Paris some of us took him to No 8 rue Colbert. He was very disgusted, and remarked, "My uncle might stay, if he came, but I'm off." None of us saw any joke, but I happened to call at the old gentleman's house the next day, and found him suffering from *gout in both thumbs*!

On another occasion he walked into a house in Paris, lazily surveyed the grinning girls, snapped out "Une douzaine de Marennes!" and made for the door. He it was who painted a number in immense characters on the door of a girl he disliked. He had at one time a small studio. Two nuns came thither a begging. Opening the door to receive them, he wittily cried "Pas de Modle" in the monotone of disgust which artists so quickly learn, and banged the door. On another occasion he caused to be printed and stuck up in all the urinoirs of the Latin Quarter the following smart satirical parody on French quack advertisements, directing it against the crapulous punk whom he also speaks of in the following pages under the pseudonym of "Sal B.....s," which I retain:

MÉTHODE B.......

TRAITEMENT TRES OFFENSIF ANIMAL

Guérison de l'impuissance dans 2 minutes
par un simple massage

PAR UNE SEULE APPLICATION
du Salecon Anglo-Négro-Hollandais:
Gonorrhée en 3 à 5 jours, Syphillis en 3 semaines
Prix de l'application: 1 franc

**ENCULMENTS: UNE SPÉCIALITE DE LA
MAISON**

**Enlèvement des fromages du prepuce
dans la salle dentaire**

---

*Et rien qu'en jetant les yeux sur le Docteur
les constipations les plus obstinées disparaissent*

**SENTEZ LE DOCTEUR ET MÉFIEZ-VOUS
DE L'IPECACUANHE!**

Cabinet (et urinoir) de Docteur 69, rue
Conpeint

I might multiply examples, but to what good purpose?

On the other hand, he would employ his fine wit in the service of piety and charity. Many are the good and generous deeds done by him under the cover of a light practical joke or quaint whim. Still less need I speak of this side of my friend; all the world knows more than I could say. His character was more than dual, however. Not only did the r of predicor vanish and return, as in the epigram of Priapus, but the devotion to literature of all kinds bore many diverse fruits. Before he was thirty he had published a volume of semi-sacred verse, a notable collection of Carmina Mariana, a short and most lucid history of the metaphysical controversies which culminated in the birth of Scholasticism, a contribution to the Encyclopaedia Britannica on some refinements of electric measurement, a series of articles on a micrococcus which he supposed himself to have discovered (his only failure, for he proved himself to be mistaken, and manfully recanted in a very honourable letter to the Editor), a short study of heraldry, which made an immense impression on the small body of thinkers who interest themselves in this curious question, and his revolutionary masterpiece upon the relation between Comparative Anatomy and Political Science.

In his personal life he had similar breadth of experience.

He was beloved of the thieves and prostitutes in an obscure drinking-cellar in Belleville, the most dangerous quarter of Paris, not as a comrade, but as a missionary. He was at home in the most exalted social circles, and it is a well-known fact that many persons of importance relied on his subtle intuition and keen vision to resolve political difficulties which baffled their less fertile brains.

Sought after by rich and poor for his personal beauty, he yielded to none, save a single boat-captain on a Seine steamer, to whom he continued faithful until his marriage. But the devotion of his young and beautiful wife exacted too much, imposed too severe a strain upon his constitution. They had been married barely a week when he took her to the infamous T.... Club in Cairo, where the dissolute officers of the Army of Occupation, merchants, fish-porters, pimps, all the cream of Egyptian society and its dregs, gathered every Wednesday night to commit appalling orgies.

He gave her to their tender mercies and saw her violated a dozen times before his eyes. In a month no more debauched woman walked the streets than this dainty English girl.

She became a mother, after innumerable adulteries on both sides, committed shamelessly in each others presence, even in spinthriae of ten or more persons; it was during the severe physical strain which her confinement imposed upon him that he wrote the Nameless Novel.

All this time of his marriage, about two years, he had been also performing miracles of piety. Ordained three years before, he rapidly gained the favour of his superiors by his modesty and eloquence. He obtained a valuable private chaplaincy in Paris, a most suitable post, allowing him plenty of leisure for other work. During this period a delicious volume of hymns came from his pen, and his self-sacrificing ministrations to the poor were the wonder of the French capital.

His evenings were spent in that witty and high-thinking informal club which met nightly at the restaurant Au Chien Rouge, whose members are so honoured in the world of Art. There he met C... the brilliant but debauched sculptor, caustic of wit, though genial to his friends; N..., the great painter, whose royal sense of light made his canvases into a harmonious dream; he also the sweet friend of Bacchus, who filled him with a glow and melody of colour and thought. There, too, were D... and L..., the one poet and philosopher, the other painter and — I fear — pederast. Twins in thought, the two were invincible in argument as they were supreme in their respective arts. Often I have sat, a privileged listener, while D...'s cold acumen and L...'s superb indignation, expressed in fiery swords of speech, would drive some luckless driveller from the room. Or at times they would hold down their victim, a bird fascinated by a snake, while they pitilessly exposed his follies to the delighted crowd. Again, a third, pompous and self-confident, would be led on by them, seemingly in full sympathy, to make an exhibition

of himself, visible and hideous to all eyes but his own. L...,
his eager face like a silver moon starting from a
thundercloud, his hair, would pierce the very soul of a
debate, and kindle it with magic joy or freeze it with scorn
implacable. D..., his expression noble and commanding, yet
sly, as if ever ready to laugh at the intricacies of his own
intellect, sat next to him, his deep and wondrous eyes lit
with strange light, while with words like burning flames of
steel he shore asunder the sophistries of one, the
complacencies of another. They were feared these two!
There also did he meet the well known ethicist, I..., fair as a
boy, with boy's golden locks curling about his Grecian head;
I..., the pure and subtle-minded student, whose lively
humour and sparkling sarcasm were as froth upon the deep
and terrible waters of his polished irony. It was a pity that
he drank. There the great surgeon, and true gentleman, in
spite of his exaggerated respect for the memory of Queen
Victoria, J..., would join in with his ripe and generous wit.
Handsome as a god, with yet a spice of devil's laughter
lurking there, he would sit and enjoy the treasures of the
conversation, adding at the proper interval his own rich
quota of scholarly jest.

Needless to say, so brilliant a galaxy attracted all the
false lights of the time. T..., the braggart, the mediocre
painter, the lusty soi-disant maquereau of marchionesses,
would seek admission (which was in theory denied to none).
But the cutting wit of C... drove him headlong, as if by the
Cherubim, from the Gates of the Garden of Eden. G..., the
famous society painter, came one night, and was literally
hounded out of the room by a swift and pitiless attack on the
part of D... and the young ethicist. A bullet-headed Yankee,
rashly supporting him, shared the same fate, and ever after
sat in solitary disgrace downstairs, like a whipped hound
outside its masters door. The subject of conversation did not
matter. A fool reveals himself, though he talk but of greasing
gimlets, in such a fierce light as beat upon the Chien Rouge.
Nor could any fool live long in that light. It turned him

inside out; it revealed him even to himself as a leper and an outcast; and he could not stand it.

In such a circle humbug could not live. Men of high intellectual distinction, passing through Paris, were constant visitors at the Chien Rouge. As guests they were treated with high honour; but woe to the best of them if some chance word let fall led D... or L... to suspect that he had a weak spot somewhere! When this happened, nothing could save him: he was rent and cast to the carrion beasts for a prey.

How often have I seen some literary or pictorial Pentheus, impious and self-sufficient as he, disguise himself (with a tremor of fear) in his noblest artistic attire, as the foolish king in the *bassara* of the Maenads!

How often have I seen Dionysus or some god discover the cheat and give him over to those high-priests of dialectic, D... and L..., to be stripped and ravaged amid the gleeful shrieks of the wit-intoxicated crowd! But once the victim was upon the altar, once he rose from his chair, then what a silence fell! Frozen with the icy contempt of the assembly, the wretch would slink down the room with a scared grin on his face, and not until he had faced that cruel ordeal, more terrible (even to a callous fool) than an actual whipping would have been, not until the door had closed behind him would the silence break as someone exclaimed "My God, what a worm!" and led the conversation to some more savoury subject.

On the other hand, there was B..., a popular painter, upon whom the whole Dog pounced as one man, to destroy him.

But when they saw that his popular painting was not he, that he had a true heart and an honest ambition, how quickly were the swords beaten into absinthes, and the spears into tournedos!

S..., again, with a face like a portrait by Rembrandt, a man of no great intellect, but making no pretension thereto, how he was loved for his jolly humour, his broad smile, his inimitable stories!

Yet it must not be supposed that the average man, however sincere, had much of a welcome there. Without intention to wound, he was yet hurt — the arrows of wit shot over his head, and he could never feel at home.

I am perhaps the one exception. Without a ghost of talent, even in my own profession — medicine — I had no claim whatever to the hospitality of the Dog. But being perfectly unobtrusive, I dare say I was easy to tolerate, perhaps even of the same value as a background is to a picture, a mere patch of neutral colour, yet serving to harmonize the whole. Certainly nothing but my silence saved me. The remark a few pages back about Hall Caine and Meredith would have caused my instant execution, by the most painful, if the least prolonged, of deaths.

Aye! no society, since men gathered together, was ever so easy to approach, to seat oneself among, to slip way from, or to be hurled in derision from their midst!

Dreaded as they were by the charlatan, no set of men could have been more closely-knit, more genial, more fraternal. United by a bond of mutual respect, even where they differed — of mutual respect, I say, by no means of mutual admiration, for it was the sincere artistry that they adored, not the technical skill of achievement — they formed a noble and harmonious group, the like of which has perhaps never yet been seen.

Of this circle K… was an honoured member. Perfectly at home in all societies, he endeared himself to this one by his singular versatility and charm, his sincerity and brilliance. Once they grasped the many-sided nature of his mind — an operation which took about two hours hard work on the part of D… and L…, for K… dissimulated, with amusing effrontery, the real harmony of his character — they knew him for a man, and loved him.

It was at the Red Dog that I first had the pleasure of meeting him. He was then living apart from his wife, who had returned to Cairo for the sake of its vice, and he occupied a small flat in the Avenue Matignon; I was myself living not far away, and about ten o'clock we left the Dog, and he suggested that I should walk home with him.

Near the Place St. Michel, however, he suddenly hailed a closed cab — it was the depth of winter — and motioned me to enter. I was exceedingly surprised, for he was fond of walking, and hated travelling in any kind of vehicle. Near the Pont-Neuf he stopped the cab, removed his great blue cloak and coat (an elaborate tunic trimmed with ermine, for he was an eccentric in costume to the point of monomania) and stepped outside with me, bidding the cabman to wait. We stood in the shadow of a large urinoir and he anxiously consulted his watch. "Dam the b...!" he exclaimed after a few minutes, "Will she trick me after all? Or has my note miscarried?"

I was more and more astonished, even embarrassed, but I dared not question him. Suddenly, however, there resounded the echo of a pitiful cry apparently proceeding from a house which stood upon the quay. A smile of pleasure chased the frown from his face. In a few moments came the sound of softly running feet upon the road, and a dishevelled woman with a face set hard like ivory dipped into the light. A movement — his strong nervous hand pressed me back — she stood upon the parapet and dived. Like a flash he was after her, and almost before I could reach the edge of the river he was swimming steadily to the steps with the unhappy girl. He bundled her into the cab with but little assistance from me, and, giving a brief excuse — and a louis — to the constable who ran up, we drove off home. He revived her with a million kisses and endearments rather embarrassing for a third party and when her eyes opened and she saw his boyish face she had only one word — "It isn't true then? Oh my God, it isn't true?" — And fell to murmuring his name with every accent of infinite love and tenderness.

At his house my astonishment was tenfold. Ready and waiting for us were hot drinks of every kind, blankets toasting before a splendid fire, a bright open bed in the luxurious room — in ten minutes he had her nude and dry and warm and happy. He dismissed me queerly: "I suppose I must follow," he laughed, lifting her tenderly into bed with yet another kiss. "I'll tell you about it one day."

So I left them. She was his mistress for more than a year — perhaps is so still. It turned out that he had spent six weeks driving the poor child, whose only folly was her love for him, to suicide, by a calculated series of abominable cruelties, above all by his refusal to return her love. The final "coup" was as I have described; he had foreseen all, provided for all.

Such incidents are characteristic of the man; he had not (I firmly believe) even the excuse of love for her.

As I have observed, the "Nameless Novel" was written during his wife's convalescence. The verses which composed the "Bromo Book" are due to many occasions. Some are mere exercises in metre. If he heard a new form of rhyme, as in the "Sailor ashore," he would compose in it, and, lest his vanity should lure him into publishing one of such exercises, he chose words which would make it impossible.

I obtained the MS. by a simple act of burglary. Being sure that he would never consent to their publication, I had no scruples for he might have destroyed them. It seems to me that the most versatile genius of this, perhaps of any age, is best served by exhibiting that genius, even where as at present, it turns to the most incredibly loathsome forms. The portrait of the Twelve Disciples would be sadly marred by so inartistic a blunder as the exclusion of Judas Iscariot.

THE NAMELESS NOVEL

PROLOGUE

"Good, by Jesus!" cried the Countess, as, with her fat arse poised warily over the ascetic face of the Archbishop, she lolloped a great gob of greasy spend from the throat of her bulging cunt into the gaping mouth of the half-choked ecclesiastic.

"It is well, my daughter, if thou art pleased," he replied, when he had swallowed the cachet of her emotions. "But my venerable pudendum asks attention." "It shall have it, father!" said the lady, and forthwith she caught his purple-knobbed pillar in her hands, and violently rubbed it in a direction perpendicular to its length, increasing both pace and pressure as the excitement of the gentleman grew more intense. But in spite of all she could do he soon ejected a small but stringy morsel of veritable sperm, which she deftly caught in her left nostril, and sniffed up, with the relish of an old buck of the Regency helping himself to snuff.

The tongue of the Archbishop had not been idle during his time; but the thoughts of his see ever interfered with his more spiritual duties, and he waxed remiss.

The Countess, sensible of the neglect, and accepting the same as a slight to her admittedly pox-eaten charms, blew off a fiery fart in his face as a slight mark of her displeasure.

It failed of its effect: on the contrary the worthy man experienced so powerful a stimulus to his erotic fancies that his shrunk penis flew violently into the air and caught the unsuspecting Countess on the point of the jaw, completely stunning her.

When he saw that she was unconscious he acted with the decision and promptitude which had raised him from a simple parish priest to the wide fame and distinction he had won. Rapidly turning her over on to her back, he opened her mouth and performed with singular verve the operation which he usually reserved till after his morning meal.

"There are more ways of killing a dog than choking it

with shit," he mused, "but none are so economical. To proceed!" Hastily cramming some of the overflow — for the Archbishop had dined well — up her nostrils, he drove a knife (which was conveniently handy) into her bowels, and plunged his straining and kicking butter-knife within the hole thus formed. The foaming guts closed round his maddened member; the convulsive heaves of the suffocated lady simulated nay, surpassed! the wildest crissations of the most accomplished courtesan, the most domesticated matrons; and the Archbishop rode to glory in a chariot of fire truly seven times hotter than its wont. Hardly had the jets of boiling love-lotion flooded the peritoneal cavity of the now rapidly putrefying Countess — the weather was hot, and she had been for some days a martyr to internal gangrene — hardly had the venerable and saintly ecclesiastic subsided with a scream, prophetic of approaching mania, upon the corpse of his victim, when the curtain was withdrawn and a reporter from the Daily M... stepped carelessly into view. His tool still dangled outside his trousers; for reporters do not wear drawers or carry handkerchiefs, and he had relieved his feelings by a juicy yet glutinous frig. Looking around the apartment he noticed the various items of interest with professional celerity, and by the time the good Archbishop had risen and repaired the disorder of his attire, he was able to bow politely and request his Grace to accord him the favour of an interview. His Grace thought the occasion insufficient; he suggested that a note in the Society column would meet all demands.

The reporter reminded him of the system of payment by the line. "I am myself paid so much a lie!" retorted the cleric, witty even after such a night as he had spent. "But I see your point!" directing a sly glance at the newsman's disordered toilet. "May I order you a closed fly?" he added with a twinkle. But the reporter was hard at work scribbling down these scintillations in short hand.

"One must live," said the Daily M...er, looking up.

"I do not see the necessity" retorted the other, straining

after originality.

"But" — a pleasanter glance overspread his face, and lit his kindly grey eyes for his own wit kept him in almost perpetual good humour — "let us say nothing of all this but what gentlemen should say. I might find it hard to explain the lady's respiratory apparatus but she could hardly account for the condition of her gigg and gut-end."

"A jammy proposition!" acquiesced the venal newsman. "A pretty spunky, turdy, mess!"

"De mort is nil nisi bonum!" insinuated the tempter.

The reporter hesitated.

"Tuam nasam in meum anum immite!" laughed the Archbishop, and the pressman, like Messrs. Pond and Morrell in Gilbert's ballad, was convinced.

"I will make it worth your while," added the wily ecclesiastic. "You shall take down in that clever shorthand of yours the true story of my life. Mr N.ch.ls will buy the book and cheat you out of the money; so there's fame and fortune at a stroke. Put away John Thomas now; permit me, pray! — Yes, a fine long battering-piece, with a nice hard chancre on the gland, I see — Oh, yes! From a water closet, certainly — look at this ulcer on my leg, I got it from a cathedral! — and we will breakfast with my boys, the goat, and the learned pig; after that we will go and see the camel fed over a cigar, after which I will run through my day's business — you shall have a couple of whores to amuse you while you wait — or you can watch my butler putting cream in the tea — his only amusement, poor fellow, I sucked him dry years ago! — and then we will sit down to a real morning's work over my reminiscences."

These, dear girl, are for you. They form this pleasant book. Now strip yourself and get a candle; lunge in front of a looking-glass and read and frig alternately. If you are grown up, a dog or a man to suck you saves labour — of any sort — and time. But I want you to swim in a perfect ocean of fuck as you read — and please God if we ever meet — what ho! I've a belly full of boiling emotion-emulsion to shoot up your Two-penny-tube, your Penny-Pipe or into your mouth, or to splash all over your bubbies, your dear fat butter-pats, your rosy-buttoned titties, or wherever you like. And when I can't spunk any more, I'll suck you off till your back aches and your eyes are blue all round, and your gallimaufry is as sore as my gully-raker will be when you've clapped me, and pissing is like passing red-hot needles, and the stricture holds my fuck back till the crisis nearly blows its top off. So now, you bitch!

CAPITULUM PRIMUM

I came from a Bottomless Pit, began the Archbishop, and I have spent my life trying to get back. No sooner had I left my mothers breast than she put me on to her clitoris, and I was hardly laid in my father's arms before his doodle was between my baby legs and jerking its creamy essence into the sunny air of Rome, where, as you may be aware, I first drew breath. I was a healthy and well-formed child; my bauble nothing remarkable, but my bollocks peculiar for their enormous size and — as it subsequently proved — the amount and quality of the fluid they were able to secrete, while my anus, fostered as you may have noticed by the wise ambition of my maternal grandmother, attained such proportions, or rather elasticity, that I believe I could accommodate the cowcatcher of a Pacific Express, or crush the life out of the diminutive and tapering jockam of a centipede. There was a crocodile once — (he sighed, and broke off. I sympathetically kept silent).

My prick, as I have hinted, was the despair of a fond but pathic uncle. In vain did he resort to rubbings of asses' milk, to decoctions herbal, mystical, medical; it was found necessary to abandon the unequal contest and to relegate my contemptible garden-engine to the category of quick firers, instead of the heavy piece of field artillery which we had hoped to produce. Its speed was indeed sufficient. At the great Gold Medal competition of the Spunk Society in 1904, I was able to satisfy no less than twenty-seven ladies, besides an exhibition frig in which I extinguished fourteen candles in sixteen attempts, thus taking the eighth prize, and special mention as the sole representative of my cloth who was able to support a child weighing fifty-six pounds on my erect lance-of-love alone, and thus accomplishing the act of sex with my hands tied behind my back. Poor little devil! As I came, she shot off my well-oiled plenipo and was immediately split up from the fork to the shoulders by the giant callibistris of Lord R...y, whose affection for a buttered bun is only equalled by the size of his Julius Caesar. This truly formidable weapon is worth a moment's digression. It hangs below the owners knees, making the kilt an unconventional, if effective, wear. In erection the noble owner can lick the cheese from under the prepuce, and Lady S...t, who has so often accommodated an ass — in the interest of bacteriologists, who had previously believed that the latter animal was not susceptible to syphilis — had declared in forcible though refined language that "it's a fair bugger, and ought to do my little Fanny's job a treat." Eulogy, you will admit, can no further go.

To return: I was a healthy and well-formed boy, and my innate stern moral sense guarded me against the temptations into which so many youngsters fall nowadays. The diminutive size of my meat-skewer baffled all the attempts of my fiery-arsed nurse, for her well-worn snatch-blatch could receive no gratification from anything smaller than a village pump-handle.

It is a singular circumstance that my relations with my god-mother (who had ad hoc taken an interest in me) were apparently of a character as pure as remote. From year's end to year's end I saw her but some half-dozen times, and on these occasions her demeanour was frigid in the extreme. It was not till later that I discovered the secret of this debauched old voluptuary. The victim of every kind of perversion from her youth up, she at last finished by obtaining the sexual orgasm only by thinking of those people with whom she was not familiar. President R.......t, E....d VII, in spite of his impotence, the Czar, the Khedive, and other poxy potentates thus fell easy victims to her lewd importunities. Malheur! in her later days she caught the King of E .....d's impotence, and was compelled to the end of her life — for the disease proved intractable to solace herself as best she could with the cold comfort of a common clicket.

Take out that bald-headed hermit! (He interrupted

himself) Whack it up! Wallop it in! What's the nanny-goat for, you pimp, if you can't go tail-twitching her hairy old tuzzy-muzzy? You shall suck the oysters out of the kidney pudding if you're good. Now — my boy!

I complied with dignity, and in a moment found the Archbishop on my back gripping my hair with one violent hand and grappling at my breasts with the other, while his sharp-beaked pond snipe tore open the folds of my wrinkled arse, ill protected by their six weeks' leaving of shit, and began pumping out its short and spitty spend with the sound of a kettle seething and crackling. Enough! I cried, and wedged a lusty turd against his tapering touch-trap. But I had to do with a past master at love's masonry. With a swift corkscrew motion of his masterly quim-stake he withdrew the opposition, and transferring it to his hand, smeared it over my face, to teach me manners, as he said.

But if he was clever, I was at least the representative of solid British doggedness. Turd after turd I launched adown my now ruptured rectum; turd after turd he withdrew, and returned to the charge. It was a strange conflict: but wit and skill must ever win against mere brute obstinacy: I resorted to finesse. Archbishop! I pleaded, clearing my mouth of the more copious portions of dung which he had so generously besmeared me, you stopped in a most interesting part of your story.

My son, you have conquered! In me the passion of vanity has ever been stronger than that of even the purest and profoundest affections. Let us continue!

He elegantly disengaged himself from my back leaving me to withdraw a weary and sodden stern-post from the accommodating gentleman's love-passage of the affectionate goat (whom I will wager my readers have forgotten, for I very nearly did). The archbishop cleared his throat and began thus. "The first real scene of passion that I ever saw was in this fashion. I had been left lone in the house one day; and, weary of confinement, I determined to stroll into the street. Not far had I gone before my attention was attracted by a small galvanized iron mission room. To my surprise, the door was ajar, and from the pulpit I heard the well known tones of a Salvation Army preacher crying 'Whosoever will may come!'"

In the centre of the hall I saw that the forms had been removed and replaced my mattresses; upon these lay my many friends in the village. I noticed Alec and Ada, Bertie and Bobine, Charles, Clara, Dick, Dora, Edward, Ethel, Frank, Fanny, George, Gertie, Harry, Herminia, Isaac, Imogen, John, Jenny, Karl, Katherine, Louis, Laura, Martin, Maud, Norman, Nellie, Octavius, Olga, Peter, Polly, Quintus, Queenie, Robert, Rosie, Samuel, Sybil, Thomas, Thais, Ulric, Ursula, Victor, Vivien, Walter, Wilhelmina, Xenocrates, Xantippe, Yeo, Yvonne, Zeno, and Zelma.

Let us lerricompoop! Said Wilhelmina, in a voice thick with lust and marred by Martin's pilli-cock, which was tickling her tonsils.

The position was now as follows:

Alec had his middle finger in Ada's eel-pot, with Bertie's man-root caught in the crook of his elbow. Also Charles' Athenaeum was held firmly in the palm of his hand by his thumb. His forefinger tickled Bobine's clitoris, and between his third and fourth fingers Dick's best leg of three vibrated. Clara's medlar got a fair share of fun out of his knuckles. With his left arm it was the same, substituting the names of Dora, Edward, Frank, Ethel, George and Fanny. Gertie and Herminia seized each one of his shoulder blades in their gaping cabbage-fields, while Imogen and Jenny were engaged with his elbow joints. Harry and Isaac had their drumsticks in his mouth; Katherine got a nose-fuck, while John and Karl had him in the arm-pits, and Louis and Martin behind the ears. Laura had his tug-mutton to her own cheek, as the saying goes, for in truth her pox eaten twat engulfed it whole. His anus accommodated Norman, while Octavius, whose wimble, though vigorous, was minute, enjoyed his umbilicus. Peter and Quintus buggered his legs, and Robert and Samuel the bend of his knee. Maud,

Nellie, Olga, Polly, Queenie and Rosie had the five toes and the heel of his left foot, while on his right were Sybil, Thais, Ursula, Vivien, Wilhelmina and Xanthippe; Yvonne and Zelma were frigging like wild things against his voluptuous patellae.

Robert, Samuel, Thomas and Ulrich goosed like good-'uns between the toes of his left foot, while Victor, Walter, Xenocrates and Yeo did the same kind office for those of his right.

Remained Zeno disconsolate; but the amorous and quick-witted lad, placing his feet together, made a capital catch-'em-alive-o for his horny flip-flap.

At the word of command the amorous assault began; at the word of command the two-and-fifty lovers came with a simultaneous yell of passion.

I found myself swimming for dear life. This is what comes, I thought, witty even in my boyhood, of the Volunteer Movement!

Why, Galahad, said my mother, how beautifully your linen is starched this week...

CAPITULUM II

My son, continued the venerable man, before I continue my affecting narrative, let me introduce you to the learned pig. This animal was trained by my old friend Lord B... and is probably the choicest gem in my collection. Approach! We approached, and the brute, contrary to all expectation, presented his rump for my inspection. After a moment's hesitation he gave a loud snort of dissatisfaction and walked to the table, from which he selected a card labelled "Kiss my arse." I drew back abashed. The engaging animal, at a sign from his master, now mounted the fattest of the venal women whom the Archbishop liked to have lying about the floor, and exposed a superb and succulent cream-stick of some fourteen inches in length. The woman lay on her back with her legs wide apart and in the air. With a bound the brute drove his sledge-hammer into her unresisting pussycat, accompanying the performance on the concertina, at both of which employments he seemed so expert that the woman beneath him squirmed with joy, and licked the snout of the monster with a lascivious tongue in her frenzy, till with a royal snort the accomplished porker, rapture dying along its verge, as Browning says of the rainbow, gave her jelly for juice, and the well-matched pair sank down in the rapture of a delicious orgasm. The concertina, falling to the floor, squeezed its air out with a long-drawn, plaintive sigh, from which an onomatopoeiomaniac Platonist who had read Cornelius Agrippa and Paracelsus would certainly have argued that the instrument had fairly frigged itself.

The animal, recovering its self-control, took a series of brass plates from the table; "Fetichist," "Sadist," "Urning," "Uranodioning," and the like from the masterly classification of John Addington Symonds. At "Masochist" the woman cried "That's me!" Master Porker lifted up his front paw and bashed her nose in. Ah! that's good! she murmured, as the clever creature sat on its hind legs and danced a most indecent "cordax dance" upon her abdomen, swollen with eight months of baby — "perhaps by the camel" whispered the Archbishop, "we shall see." A bright idea struck him, as the dance, appreciated as it was, did not instantly cause a recurrence of the orgasm. He picked out "Coprophile." With a yell of pleasure the girl-mother called on him to do his dirtiest. He complied. From his dripping schnickel frothed a hot stiff stream of greenish piss at an incalculable pace, while from his pink arse dripped the faeculent and pultaceous turdlings which we associate with a diet of wash.

The stench was intolerable. Minute by minute passed by, and still the unsurpassed bladder of the unclean animal of the Semite and the Mussulman shot out its hissing torrents. Her greedy mouth frothed and seethed with the o'erflowing billows; for the poor lass's throat, do what she might — and she had done her best to swallow many a slimestick, thereby noticeably enlarging the passage — was still too small to dispose of the formidable current of urine with which her too complaisant lover now furnished her. Her merkin too dripped over the odd ends of the champion stool. "The gospel hall is full" whispered the Archbishop. "They will have to hold an overflow meeting in the arsehole."

Sure enough, the delicate-minded girl now turned her attention to the part in question. By her incomparable gift of suction, which years of practice and not a little natural aptitude had bestowed upon her rectum, she absorbed the bulk of the faeces; while any unconsidered trifles stuck in her abundant and curly pubic hair. I could not restrain my enthusiasm, or my thorn-in-the-flesh from bursting my fly — the buttons were but carelessly sewn on, for my mother was too randy with the sly sucks I was bestowing upon her accidentally-exposed clitoris to pay strict attention to the less fascinating pursuits of the seamstress. Laying hold of its resilient vigour I shouted, "Give me that arse, O pig of pigs!" The well-trained animal produced a card "Whose?"

I was in a dilemma. I had meant the girl's, of course, but to say so now would be to affront, possibly even to enrage, one for whom I had a deep respect. On the other hand, to offer my favours to him would be to lose the supreme suction of the lady's turd-hole. I finessed again. The girl's eyes were still smarting from the acrid urine of her four-footed friend, and it was with tolerable certainty of impunity from discovery that I pointed to my chancre and to the plate "Masochist." The pig picked up his concertina. "Too late, or else too early" he played with intense, wistful sadness, pointing with the tail of his eye to the bookshelf where stood a treatise on Syphilis, which pointed out but too clearly that the only proof of cure was re-infection.

But the Archbishop's vanity was aroused; he saw that I was losing interest in himself; and this was no part of his plan. Dashing into the arena he frigged himself violently into the air, catching the gobs of sperm with great dexterity and tossing them up like a juggler, while moulding them little by little into a solid mass. He did not stop until (in one hundred and eighty two orgasms) he had collected seven balls of about four ounces each, which he kept gaily spinning in the air, and then hurling them with unerring accuracy at the exposed cabbage-patches of his numerous lady friends. "Come" he said, rising, with a sad sweet smile, "to our reminiscences! This is weary work."

CAPITULUM III

I was some seven years old, resumed the Archbishop, at the close of the exciting interlude described in the last chapter, when I first obtained any real satisfaction from the passion of love, which has since done so much to regulate and inspire my career. The incident occurred on this wise. For some days my ponderous and unwieldly bollocks had become turgid and swollen with the fluid we know, my boy, you dog! as spunk. Eighty-three pounds and four ounces they weighed on the penny-in-the-slot machine at our village station, and had it not been for the singular robustness of my physique, unenervated by debauch, I should have seen myself condemned to share the unenviable lot of the Samoan with elephantiasis of the scrotum, and support my too generous endowments with a wheelbarrow. Fortunately this extreme measure was not required, but for all that the fullness of these giant sperm-sacks caused me no little inconvenience at such games as football and the like. Occupied with my trouble, which modesty forbade me to reveal even to my parents, I wandered, nursing with thoughtful hands the bags of fecundity, in the park belonging to one of our local magnates, a famous distiller of old Scotch whisky, and reputed in venereal circles as a grand trencher man at a mutton-pie. But I was destined to unmask this fellow. He was, as I speedily discovered, but a worn-out reprobate, a fellow of Fumbler's Hall, a mere butterfingers at coney-catching! In a dingle of one of his numerous bosky dells, I came upon this fellow, boozing at a bottle of his own vile fusel-oil, and encircled by a group of naked whores, who amused themselves by protracted efforts to induce his shrunken tarse to assert itself. They were in vain. The Weary Willie of the incompetent gut-grinder remained supine for all they could do. And they did their best. None of them were out for an airing, in racing phrase. I learned later that their pay depended absolutely on their success with his much-abused affair. In vain they exposed the most fascinating parts of their anatomy; in vain their well-oiled hands, their mouths greasy with each others' spendings creamy or mucous, strove with the inexorable arbitrament of Nature: the warrior hid his bashful head, and no god altered the dread fiat, uttered even below half-cock: Thus far, and no farther! My own modest arbor-vitae, though, as you may guess, shared no such disabilities. Advancing, I showed its quiet dignity to the first lady. This woman, who had so great an influence upon my after life, merits a few words of description. By race a full-blooded negress, by profession a three penny-uprighter, by education a woman of singular charm and spirituality, by inclination a sapphist and cock-sucker, by disease a barrel, she was as delicious a rabbit-pie as I ever laid this knife to. Over six feet in height, she measured even more around her waist, owing to a dropsy on the one hand, and on the other to the presence in her uterus of a constant stream of elderly gentlemen engaged in a futile search for their headgear.

Her black and ulcerated titties dropped sweat and pus. They were of enormous size, and stuck out impudently in front of her. Her navel was like a rat-pit, and in its corrugations strange insects crawled. Her square push beggars description. Yet I must essay it in the interests of your readers, my son. Gaping like the crater of some active volcano, with a constant stream of gleet oozing from the raw and meaty orifice, it was (to complete the illusion) crowned by a light cloud of smoke, doubtless given off by the last gentleman's love-spunk. The pubic hair was ragged, and the skin torn as if by the ravages of lice and fingernails. But the anus made up for the same, for the shit sticking to the hair had well manured the growth, which was in some places more than two feet long, curling over in billows. But there was more to that quim than may appear on the surface. Vast and cumbrous as it appeared, at the first glimpse of my juvenile and at no time big twat-teaser, she screwed up the jaws of her rat-trap so that I subsequently (as you shall hear) had the utmost difficulty in effecting a lodgement. You have not long to wait, for excited by the voluptuous spectacle she afforded, I rushed upon her with my plug, like a ravening and a roaring lion. She caught me in her black and hairy arms, and gently commenced to chew my tender lips and to mouth them with her masses of blubber. At the same time she denied me any entrance to her secret charms. In vain I lubricated the threshold of the sanctuary with my young and semi-liquid baby-juice; in vain I plunged, like a kicking horse, against the succulent bivalve. The laughter of the others maddened me: the astuteness which has ever served me, which has made me what I am, came to my aid. I banged with my hangers upon the perineum. Fart after fart testified to the internal commotion so formidable an attack could not but produce in the lady's dropsical guts: profiting by a moment of slackness on her part, a second of unwary relaxation, and the resounding plop of my boyish belly gainst her mangy mount of Venus testified that I had taken advantage of her swiftly-repented oversight. But I won all too dearly the amorous victory. Caught in the vice of her hypertrophied constrictor cunni, I was now unable to move the lower part of my body, and my no longer serviceable balls drooped helplessly from their suspender. The pressure of her lousy but expert weather-gig gave me excruciating agony: for it was impossible even to work in order to produce ejaculation, on which I naturally relied to gain my point. But not for nothing had I been trained in the School of Mines! (I thought you were at this time but seven years old, I ventured. He seemed not to hear.) By pulling at her bubbies by their nipples, which were an excellent grip, I was able to start a swinging movement, whose aim the charming but unscientific girl did not suspect. In a few moments my ponderous balls were again thundering on her already weakened isthmus, and at the same time I was gathering myself, excited by the voluptuous nature of the struggle, for a stupendous effort. My chance came at last: the tow-wow relaxed its agonizing pressure, and in one rush of boiling tapioca pudding I emptied my eighty odd pounds into her cloak-room, drowning three innocent old gentlemen, and the maid who looked after their hats and sticks. It was too much for her capacity: the internal pressure of so much liquor neutralized that of her now wearied india-rubber-plant, and I was able at leisure to achieve the fourteen fucks and a dry-bob which I had originally contemplated. Amid the plaudits of the entire assembly I withdrew my dripping banana from her now yawning grease-hole, and with a flourish of my hat and an exaggerated bow to the company, I withdrew, having fairly (I think you will admit) won my spurs on the field of battle.

Were you knighted on the field? I now dared to inquire, seeing him silent.

No, you young suck-shit, he answered genially, but I was bloody well poxed.

CAPITULUM IV

Shortly after the conclusion of the events which I so lusciously described in the last chapter, continued the Archbishop, I was the means, under heaven, of saving the life of a valued member of society. The whisky-distiller had many connections in the Highlands of Scotland, and no doubt the story of my exploit enlivened many a dull wet night in that dreariest of countries. Anyhow, one day my father came down from his office in a state of appalling excitement, waving a telegram. He masturbated four times in his anxiety to control his feelings, and let us have the news, which when read seemed as bald and colourless as the pee-hole of an albino baby. But there was a hidden meaning. The telegram read simply: Self incapacitated by overwork B.lm.r.l commandeered can no more hear you can help majesty starving future Empire at stake. Brown.

It was from the famous John Brown!

My father was a man of action: in twelve hours I was admitted at the gates of B.lm.r.l by the last survivor of what had been the gallant 72nd. The G.rd.ns had perished to a man the day before, and the Bl.ck W.tch, loyal to the death, had barely lasted through the morning. I was pulled, rather than led, by the despairing maids of honour into the royal bedchamber. By the bed the P....e of W...s with dogged heroism, game and grit to the last, was lifting for the final effort his fantastically-tattooed bean-tosser upon the stupendous crinkum-crankum of the Imperial fuckstress. Hourly bulletins were being anxiously issued by the stern and pale-faced doctors, the sole unworn males within a hundred miles. The telegraph was wearing out: troops were rushed Northward: Mr B......k was mobilising his Army corps, but it was not the imagination alone of a footler that could ease the distinguished sufferer: it was solid marrow-bone she wanted, and tons of it at that.

I toddled to the bed — remember I was not yet eight

years old! Throwing a leisurely leg over the whisky-sodden mass of fat that Britons called their Q...n, I called Time! and began. The slippery and lax bung-hole of the flatulent monarch was ill-suited to my boyish chink-stopper: but Love will find a way, and the head surgeon hastily ligatured its tapering delicacy to the protuberant and pendulous clitoris of the royal patient. Ten minutes later he was able to announce to the joyful crowd that the temperature had not risen further, and that under God England might owe the restored health of the nymphomaniac to the attentions of the hitherto despised Frenchman. The news was flashed over the country, and the people breathed again. But the issue hung long in doubt. With what care did I husband the spunky torrent I lavished in such wanton profusion upon my first love, the dropsical negress! Drop by drop I distilled love's essence into that clinging carnal-trap: fuck by fuck I doled out to her the resources of my boyish liver-turner: hour after hour passed in stern and heroic effort, and yet the fever was but slightly abated. The crisis was not over! At eleven o'clock on the following morning a cheer announced the arrival of the Sc.ts G..rds, and they unstrapped me for a meal and a drink while the doomed regiment filled the breach. But the respite was of short duration. Thrice in the afternoon did cavalry regiments thunder in: thrice the corpses of them all, men and horses, were rolled down the marble staircase. By seven in the evening I was again in request. I was furious at the irony of my lot, for the corpse of a guardsman had caught my childish fancy, and the kingdom of England might have gone to hell for me — I would rather have been strapped to the dead man's shako than wallow for a week in the royallest Busby in Christendom. But I had passed my word. I resumed the now distasteful task. She has been like this for a month (I heard the Head Surgeon whisper to the German Ambassador, who had ventured to make his enquiries with his Master John Thursday, or schmeichaz, as he himself would have called it, done up in a solid steel case as a measure of precaution.) —

John Brown gave up after ten days or so, and since then —
he spread his hands in despair and the sweat trickled down
his cheeks.

Yes; it was up to me, and no mistake. Terrible news came
from the South: one of the finest regiments in the service had
refused to obey the order to proceed North: another had
thrown down its arms, and tossed off as one man. Yet a third
was so worn by its debauchery with the gilded youth who
haunt the Knightsbridge bars that the jury of matrons who
examined them decided that to hurry them North was to
waste the railway fares, and to raise false hopes in the
nation. It was up to me!

Luckily, I was up to it. Hour after hour my gaudy
bollocks jerked their wiry emissions into the apparently
insatiable cut-and-come-again of this hot-arsed bawdy-
basket. Night after night, with short intermissions at the
arrival of a posse of constables or a naval contingent, did I
plunge upon that flabby doodle-sack: but the champion
pizzle-skinner of the World was not to be toyed with by a
boy of not yet eight years old! The mouth thankless
swallowed all my hoarded spendings and asked, shrieked,
yelled, for more. On the sixteenth day I was feeling weak
toward morning, and the sufferer, albeit a shade less eager,
had not perceptibly slackened. The surgeon's hair, greyed in
the first week, was now falling out in handfulls. The stench
of so many unburied corpses was becoming intolerable. My
erstwhile well-hung cods sagged wearily against the lower
portion of the Imperial slit: and only the loyal assistance of
the maids of honour in supporting and swinging my body
kept me at all to my duty. Fuck me! hoarsely whispered the
gin-smelling potato-trap of the still randy sovereign. I
screwed up my almost deliquescing tickle-toby to the pitch
of another jumble-giblets, but it was with no hopeful
outlook. Frankly, to myself — and the surgeons read my
gloomy thought — I was compelled to look facts in the face,
and admit that a very few hours now would see me sink a
corpse at the very breach in which so many brave men had

fallen fighting. For I was determined not to withdraw, even if the lady herself had been willing to let me off. This she was not. Her greasy and rotund arms held me to her bulging belly, the bloated and ill-smelling butter-bags flopping down with fat, their black nipples inflamed with lust and alcohol. Her bristly scut scraped my boyish abdomen; her spunk-besmeared grummet stuck ever closer to my ever wearier rubigo. So I made the best of a bloody bad job, and gave her a spirit-indeed-is-willing-but-the-flesh-is-weak prick-scouring as if the last trump were going to sound in a minute, and I were afraid to be "caught with my work half done on Judgement Day," as Browning says.

So I leather-stretched wearily on.

During all this time the Empr.ss had kept up her strength by copious libations of whisky, (which stood in casks at a great height above her head, and trickled down in tubes into her royal mouth, on the same principles as saline injections). But I suppose the violence of her paroxysms or the mechanical effect of so much-needed respite while the lady vomited quart after quart of most noxious bile and spirits upon the bed. For nearly an hour she retched and strained, giving off putrid farts and eructations as of a dyspeptic sow, while the sticky and purulent sweat ran over her blubber flanks. But at the expiration of that time, she was again ready for action, and indeed, seemed to be so set on edge by her involuntary abstention that I doubt whether after all I gained much by the interruption.

How's the hot poultice for the Irish toothache? I whispered to the gluttonous and open-arsed schickster. Shit! she sighed; shut your mug and open your urethra, and get on with the bum tickling, can't you? (I give you my word I had not spoken for three days and more.) But argument is proverbially vain with a woman in the middle of a rousing bacon-rubbing. I blocked steadily on. In vain I had cudgelled my wits to find some substitute for the fatiguing exercise of rumping; but the surgeon warned me that the suggestion would be taken in ill part. Her Majesty, he explained, is before all things respectable: not to save life, no! not to ensure the greatness of her empire or the happiness of her people, would she for a moment condescend to any unnatural practice such as you suggest. I am aware that a number of horses have perished in the service; but I can certify that our distinguished patient was not at the time in a condition to differentiate between the steed and its rider. What she wanted was live sausage for supper, and plenty of gravy; now the worst is over — thanks greatly to your noble exertions, which I implore you to continue, and not to offend our English ears, and corrupt our English minds, with the practical but improper suggestions of the degraded foreigner. She is now in a condition to understand what is said, and your remark that you see no moral difference between the employment of a horse and a motor car would, at a time when your services were less necessary than at present, expose you to the gravest reprimand from the Censor of Plays, or possibly the London County Council, while I myself as a scientist should feel obliged to remind you that in the present state of our knowledge we are not acquainted with any means by which the motor car is able to reproduce its species. So he spoke, while I laboured at the foaming oyster-catcher before me. I was now — it was the fifteenth day since the last relief party had fallen, for all England was now up in arms against what their freeborn spirit considered an uwarrantable and tyrannical demand on their manhood — it is a good thing, said George W.....m himself, to have a giant's strength, but tyrannous to use it like a giant — while the sporting instinct of the race was equally aroused, and they were as one man (so the Pink 'Un voiced the generous feeling of the community) in their resolve "to stand away, and let's see the Frenchy have his whack out" —I was now, in the words of the sweet singer of Israel, faint yet pursuing, (I was but a boy!) when a yell of rage, like that of a famished tiger, resounded through the palace. Dashing aside all opposition, passive though it was, for the waiting-women could not get out of the way quickly enough, there rushed into the room a dark and gigantic mass of brawn. I was torn, regardless of the ligature, from my unsavoury perch, flung, in spite of my tender years, to the floor, and with a roar like the crash of an universe in its death-pang, a vast and hairy gut-stick plunged into the yawning abyss which the lobster-pot of the gluttonous Guelph offered to its raging lust. Instantly a volley of viscous baby-juice spurted from the loose corners of the now delighted whim-wham, and a yell of obscene bawdy-talk from the crapulous and fuck-sodden mouth of the Imperial buttock-broker appraised my all but succumbing senses that my job was over. At the moment of collapse I had been saved from utter rout and open shame. John Brown had come back to his own.

And his own received him! chuckled the Archbishop at the conclusion of this historic section of his memoirs, during the recital of which I had been so excited that I had repeatedly been obliged to solicit the favours of the Ecclesiastic's beautiful goat, whose congenial jelly-bag completed my practical sympathy with the story.

Come! continued the Archbishop, we will stroll across to the camel. My arse is thirsty for a drain of fuck as ever your Fleet-Street throats are for a two of Scotch.

I will only remark, to round off your chapter, that Her Majesty has ever been sensible of my efforts to please, and that it is due to her that I owe my introduction to a clerical career, and the proud station in the realm which I, although by birth a foreigner, have the honour to occupy. But my farter burns for a pisser, and I see Hassan (so I call the dear beast) has a stand like the tower of Pisa. Come, and I'll suck you off as we go.

CAPITULUM V

It is a singular circumstance, continued the Archbishop, leading the way across the piles of dung with which the devoted camel had adorned the floor, that no poet has yet adequately sung the passion which exists in such luscious splendour between the "Ship of the Desert" and the wild Bedawi. Leila, the juicy-cunted nigger nockstress who took my first spunkings as I told you in Chapter III, used to see a great deal of the business when she was first brought up from her home by the Nyanza to serve the vices of George G....n at Khartoum. She had seen Mesrur, the famous eunuch of the Mahdi, violate the hairless cunnies of sixty virgins without losing erection. She had been present when Zuleika, the Queen of the Soudan, as they called her, undertook (to suck off, and swallow the spend of) fifty-seven men in the first hour, and seventy-two in the second, when she had got into her stride, as it were. Alas! all Europe knows the treachery which cost her life. In the third hour the infamous Selim bin Haroun presented himself disguised to her hasty lips. As you know, this chieftain, desirous of checking his fertility without interfering with his pleasures, had bored a hole at the root of his life-preserver permitting the vital fuck-spunk to dribble away. Of course, when the unhappy Zuleika pulled at his vibrating tuning-fork and found that no juice followed her efforts, she shrieked and fainted, suspecting magic. Recovering herself by a great effort, she caught hold of the traitor's bollocks, and went on. For three minutes and a half she continued to suck him with her whole force; he reeled, fell, and expired. Zuleika was avenged. But for all her gallantry the Amir was adamant. Your engagement was to average over fifty cocks an hour (he said) and you have failed; the penalty is known to you. The unhappy woman groaned and acquiesced. The eunuchs stuffed a vast quantity of rice into her front and back paddy-fields, and with delicate enemata of boiling water caused it to swell. They stood away at the critical moment, and with a yell like ten thousand devils in torment the bowels of the wretched woman burst open and she expired in frightful agony.

The recital of this scene of lust, said the Archbishop, always moves me to tears. See! And his tapering phallus was again the scene of a brilliantly conceived and admirably executed frig. Yes! resumed the emotional ecclesiastic, she had seen many a sight which if it were graven with a needle on the eye-corners, were a warning to such as would be warned. She was present when George G.rd.n was violated by seventy-eight dervishes in seventy-eight separate spear-wounds: her vade-mecum had vibrated to the lusty rolling-pins of Sir H......t S.....t's column in the dusty square of Abu-Klea: she had held up the dying hero's head with her black knees and received the last spending he ever spent this side of Heaven in her capacious mouth. She, and she alone, had avenged Arabi Pasha, when on the stricken field of Tel-el-Kebir, she pitched her cunt and poxed eleven thousand Tommies in one night. She was the veteran who stood by statued Memnon at sunrise, and with the music of her farts out sang the storied stone. She, uncrowned Empress of mankind, she, carrion of a million stallion men, she was my love, my dove, my undefiled! To me, the mere boy bugger of the Bay of Biscay, this peerless rantipole offered the squittery slime of her arse-gut and the slithery spunkings of her force-pump, as well as the no less fuck-smoothed dumb-oracle, her blubber potato-trap.

To me! To me! To me all the juicy gamahuches of the morning!

To me the fucks that give one zest for lunch! To me the buggerings of the early afternoon, and the bub and armpit joys that occupy the wise from five o'clock to dinner. To me the nameless raptures of the evening and the night! O fucking! what fun you are!

"Sweet, when the morn is grey;
Sweet, when they clear away
Lunch, and at close of day
Possibly sweetest."

But I am forgetting. The passion of the wild Bedawi for his untiring steed is indeed a theme for the noblest of poets. Here — he indicated the camel Hassan with an airy wave of the hand, at the same time within comparable dexterity directing the vast battering-ram into, and engulphing it within, his pile-ridden and fistula-riddled bung-hole — is a camel. See with what joy he plunges in my turd-pipe! How his love-lobes bang against my bum! How he spurts his Scotch Broth into my very colon! — By the way, did I ever tell you how the K..g of E.....d missed his coronation? — I shook my head and the tip of my Timothy-tool in negation. It was thus, continued the Archbishop, while the camel still played the part of Captain Shaw, a type rather of true love let loose than kept under, sending his foaming cream, like an advertisement of a shaving-stick, into the steaming guts of the enthusiastic celibate. King E....d, while yet P....e of W...s, had, as you know, indulged in every form of vice. But no! Though the plug-tail of Fred A....r and many another has sought every cranny of his natural orifices, every pox-hole of his worm-eaten flesh, every fat-fold of his obese person, yet his happiness was to be threatened, his faith in the Order of Things shaken, his whole soul thrown upon a novel and doubtful enterprise, and that at a moment when it might have been thought (go on, Hassan!) that Heaven itself had no more to offer him.

It was one day of Spring at W.nds.r. Mrs Arthur P...t lay in a bath of sticky sperm, not P...t's, not the K...g's! Whose, then, you ask? The sticky sperm of Kluckchoo, the Human Corkscrew.

Fresh from his laurels at the Empire, the Human Corkscrew had been commanded to appear before the K..g. If he can do that with his body, what will he not be able to do with his prick? thought the witty little woman, the worthy pupil of Immanuel Kant. She fitted act to deduction, and an hour after the performance the trouble-giblets of Kluckchoo was worming about in the universally admired cunnikin of the fashionable nestlecock. His complaisance was however not without reason. Tell your old fumble monger, said he when her delirium was appeased, that I can give him a new sensation, and one of such delight that he will never have experienced the like, nay! Nor the shadow of it. Do that to me, dear heart! cried the randy Moll Muckmeabart. Not I, said the expert, you would not get up for three days and more: such is the pleasure. This made her only the keener, and when he saw that she would cry a rape unless he consented — "and you must see, darling, how necessary it is for anyone in my position to be able to do that at any moment — the witnesses are all ready, and you would not stand a chance!" — he abandoned the unequal contest; and the unique performance of Kluckchoo, the Human Corkscrew, began.

The jargonelle of this wonderful man merits a careful description, but I am so tired of dictating this rotten book, so anxious to devote myself as closely to this sweet beast as he is devoted to me, that you will get but a perfunctory one. It had all the qualities of the pseudopodia of the Amoeba. Get out your Marshall and Hurst, and read up Amoeba, and you will know as much as I do.

Little by little he advanced this engine into the palpitating cavity of the bona roba both by front and rear. Her uterus soon filled up, but for one and a half hours the giant tentacle of the wily Kluckchoo pressed up her hairy arsehole, and filled her greasy guts to bursting. Groping about in the dark with his exquisitely sensitive and perfectly trained tool, he at last found the lady's Appendix, into the narrow orifice of which he pushed voluptuously, and there spunked out his love-lap.

The spending anonyma fainted with pleasure, and the cautious Kluckchoo withdrew, only to be summoned in all haste to the royal apartments three days later, when Mrs

Arthur disclosed her find to her keeper.

To make a long story short, the K..g was so delighted with the Appendix-fuck of Kluckchoo, that he did absolutely nothing else all day and all night. Affairs of state went by the board, and to the cringing official who dared to remind him of his approaching coronation, he replied: Bugger the Coronation! This language shocked the prudish English, and damaged the K..g's popularity in Nonconformist circles. His surgeons took a heroic course.

While the royal pathic lay in the delirious trance of Kluckchoo's emissions, they chloroformed him, and removed the little sac whose naughtiness had so nearly destroyed the Coburg loaf. When the K..g was made sensible of his loss his fury was terrible: but the effect of a long convalescence, abstinence, and tonics was to produce a cockstand or its semblance in his shrunken anatomy. Lady B....e, displaying the magnificent rolls of her saucy spleuchan in his face, completed the conquest. The K..g smiled again. England was saved! But o Q...n A.......a! was it fair to those who had resuscitated your royal consort's drooping dolly from an early grave to rush in as you did, get astride the now standing leather-stretcher of the dilapidated monarch, catch it in your grey, your scraggy, your mucus-dripping, your cold and stale-smelling cellar-door, and by the furious heaves of your skinny buttocks release that greasy fountain which you could never have done by the honest pressure of your flabby Dripping Well of Knaresborough? No, queen though you may be, an honest man condemns you to your face. The bit of stiff was Lady B....e's and T....s should have been allowed to swallow the sex sauce, whereas you, haughty and selfish woman, cheated her tar bucket with your shrivelled crab-apple, while, miser to the last, you took his perquisite to chew at your leisure with your minions, the dirty scavengers that gold still seduces to dip their luckless coney-catchers in the scabby duckpond that the Q...n of E.....d called her privy Paradise...

The Archbishop's enthusiasm had overpowered him.

Impaled upon Hassan's engine, and supported by the teeth of the now thoroughly excited beast, he had fainted: but the camel's joy-junket still spurted through the fistulae of that bubbling arsehole, and with a long and regular swing the Ship of the Desert continued his fascinating exercise.

The Archbishop will go on like this all night, said a sweet voice behind me. I turned, and saw Leila, the black-bumboed-blouzabella of his boyhood. Come with me, she added, I can still beat you at cuddle-my-cuddie. She saw me hesitate, but a gob of spew in my left eye convinced me that her desires were really aroused by my charms. I spat back at her, and watched the greasy morsel trickle down the open ulcer that spread across her left cheek, and had eaten away her nose and half a lip. She caught me up to her and smeared the pus into my mouth. In a sort of rapture she stowed me away in her fuck-sodden snatch-box, and rushed to her bedroom, there no doubt to initiate me into the joys of love, as known among these bawdy-minded buttered buns, and nowhere else, unless in your hearts, my dainty girls that read this book. Eh?

CAPITULUM VI

I think, said Leila, as her frantic dripping-pan release my frizzling sausage, done to a turn, that we shall restore your despondent tickle-gizzard to a better condition if we look on a bit at the Archbishop, and his games. Surely he is asleep after such a night with the camel, I objected, for it was now morning, the expert melting-pot of the hot-arsed hogoninny having kept my metal at the point all night without ever giving it a chance to run over. Not he! she sneered. He is now with his Venerable Aunt, as he calls her, a lascivious old woman if ever there was one! A very gobble-prick! A brimstone bunter! But come! You shall see them.

We strolled into the next room, where the grey-haired old foreskin-hunter was in the very act of swallowing the large and luscious semolina pudding that trickled from the recently frigged whore-pipe of her nephew.

Two active boys were engaged in stuffing her lucky-bag with current numbers of the Daily M..., as I observed with satisfaction, guessing at last the secret of our enormous circulation.

When the supply of these was done, they continued with the Sunday S....d and that peculiarly foul organ, Good W...s.

This was her chief pleasure, since she had sought this temporary retirement from the whirl of politics. Licking her loose and wrinkled lips, she spat the glutinous relics of her nephew's emission into the face of her last lover, a Scotch missionary of a bloated and drunken type, and began her favourite anecdote, the story of her election as a Dame of the Grand Council of the P......e League. To skip irrelevant details, she began, let me merely say that I was stripped and whipped by a bevy of lust-maddened wagtails, headed by a Marchioness. My unfailing sense of propriety led me to protest against this unmeaning assault: but in vain.

A string of girls and women seized my clitoris —
(I saw this now for the first time. What I had supposed to

be a coil of rope on which she was sitting slowly arose and unwound itself. It was a clitoris indeed! Lady's love-lump were a futile term: rather a fancy-fagot's fuck-flapper, in Sw.nb.rne's faultless phrase. But all phrases are weak. It was Nature's standing miracle.) — which, as you will observe, is ninety-seven yards, two feet, and four and three quarter inches in length — it is the sorrow of my life that I have never touched the 100 yard mark! — and standing in a long row, began to frig and suck it madly. As you can see, I can coil and uncoil it at pleasure: I can wind myself up in it: I could hang myself in it if the whim took me. I have dipped it in treacle, and given a Sunday-School treat which the children will remember for years — they all got the clap! — I have smeared it in birdlime, and caught a record lot of eagles: I have buggered eight pythons at one moment: I have — But why boast, she piously interrupted herself, since it is but the grace of God? Yet, for His Glory, I proceed. I have used it to climb the most inaccessible rocks: the Mittleggi Grat of the Eiger, the N. face of the Matterhorn, the E. face of the Zinal-Rothhorn, whose last 50 feet baffled the unequalled Bletzerstoch; all, all have fallen before the dauntless dexterity by which I have thrown up its sensitive end, and hauled myself up laboriously after it. I have used it to save the lives of gallant British tars when the lifeboat overturned, and the Rocket apparatus jammed; for I flung it aboard the distressed ship in the teeth of a fearful gale, and held it there for hours while the grateful seamen swung to land in buckets. I have also, she continued more shyly, derived some gratification of a sensual nature from its employment. But nothing to the P......e League! They got there, and they stayed there: they stayed there till the poor old emotion-knob was nearly torn to shreds. The Conservative Female is a pretty randy proposition, you bet your life!

But enough of my election! (she broke off as suddenly as she had begun, for she was of a low type of intelligence, and constant tippling had undermined her rudimentary brain), let us fuck a bit! Let us spunk! Let us come! Why don't you lick me, Bertie? Stuff some more rags up, Harry! Now, Archbishop, can you give me a good soaking mouthful of your pleasure-pudding? —

But I had seen enough. Leila's hand and the voluptuous orgie before me had completed the convalescence of my invalid lollipop; and with a yell of lust I flung myself upon her eternally open gravy-giver. The Archbishop and his dirty-minded old aunt were blotted out as the water-closet of my black judy sent its gushes of pus and hotchpotch over me, and gripped Old Slimy with its marvellous clutch.

Oh girls! She was a grand fuck! May you all be but a thousandth part as kind to your lovers, and you will never want for a meaty girlometer to make you a baby, or to bid you wallow in the randier emotions of a sterile spend.

I learnt later from the Archbishop that his Venerable Aunt was a noteworthy figure in her way. She it was who conceived the idea of taking a Webster's Unabridged Dictionary and erasing the name of anything which could not be introduced into her thatched house, or rubbed against or wrapped round her wonderful clitoris. She then steadily and conscientiously worked through the list thus obtained. After years of severe and indefatigable toil she was able to announce the epoch making conclusion (which philosophers had guessed without ever proving by a truly scientific method) that there was nothing like a cock for fucking, and that a tongue was the best thing in the world for sucking off. Her classical researches have encouraged a host of other investigators to engage in similar tasks, and thus stimulated all that is best in modern civilization to probe the immense mysteries that ever ring in our puny intelligences, our befogged and poxy brains. The digression has been long, but I trust not without edification; and in our next chapter you may rely on our returning to the story of the Archbishop's early life, and his romantic career in the Latin quarter with S...y B.....s and the Frigging Photographers.

CAPITULUM VII

Only for one short period, resumed the Archbishop, no whit exhausted by his previous efforts, did I turn from the clerical career which the Q...n's kindness opened to me. But the restrictions of the training were at first as irksome to me as they were to Fra Lippo Lippi in Browning's immortal poem, and Art seemed a halfway house. Suiting the action to the thought, I soon found myself in Paris, and rooms in a dirty little basement in the Montparnasse Quarter. My next-door neighbours were photographers, one, by name L..s, calling himself an artist, and his partner H...s, pluming himself upon his business capacity. L..s was the son of a charlatan parson once well known in England as a mountebank, while his mother, disgusted that he was a boy, brought him up as a girl, as far as she possibly could. He even slept with her till he was eighteen: and we may guess the result.

H...s was a snivelling shit. L..s wore long hair, never washed and rarely shaved. His pictures were beneath criticism, and his manners — Mean little skunks, the slimy pair of them!

Now in an attic in the same building lived S...y B.....s, the common road of the quarter: an illustration of Euclid's position that the Hole is greater than its Quarter. This was a dirty split-arse mechanic with nigger blood peeping through her low-caste white parentage. She smoked an inordinate number of cigarettes per diem, and her teeth and breath told the tale. She opened her skinny legs to anything in the shape of a tent-peg that she could catch hold of, and drag unwilling to her lousy and pox-eaten touch-hole. She had long been L..s' bit of fish, and now shared him with H...s. But they frigged most of the time, for the stench of S...y's cabbage was too niffy even for the nose of L..s, and their roots were hardly capable of a decent stand. Such specimens of worms I never hope to see or smell again, and I trust that you will forgive my polluting your ears, journalist though you are, with such noisome stuff. (*I can vouch for the faithfulness of this description, for I know the swine well enough, and in no other than a book of filth would I have introduced any one of the three. Ed.*) My artistic studies progressed but slowly, for much of my time was occupied with a liaison I had formed with Stephen Jimson, to whom the Ode (infra) is addressed. This youth had the peculiar facility of spotting sodomites in the most unlikely places. He would in a short walk along the boulevard recognize as confreres in homosexual vice some ninety-five percent of the passers by.

He was not happy unless he felt that he had an arsehole into which he could run for shelter from the cold world at a moment's notice. He wanted to feel that he had but to crook his middle finger, and nine-inch nockers would come running up by the thousands to grope their little Stevie's brown crack. I loved his coarse-skinned handsome face; I sucked with considerable élan his fine but overworked sugar-stick; I pumped the rare but treacly semen from his gland; I wallowed in the inkstand of his arse. I mixed my prolific spunk with his not less abundant shit: in brief, we loved.

The happy days fled all too fast in mutual masturbation, in pure buggery, in all the arts of the successful sodomite.

I thrill at this very hour with the sweet memory of those happy careless days. My prickle, my jolly little pizzle, my dainty Davy, my vimmy little Ox in a Teacup, my blessed little bag-of-tricks, was ever on the qui vive for a punk's cuntlet, and a good old go at Cully-shangy. But now — He broke off and shed a silent tear. Reaching for a honey-pot, by which I here mean an actual jar of real china containing the saccharine produce of the really truly bee, he dipped his nervous nilnisitando into the glucose mass, and withdrawing, leant back and wearily chewed ginseng, while he cooled his throat with a strong infusion of Cantharides in old brandy. I am not what I was, he grumbled. These tales of my youth weaken me. Since the Countess called — rot her rasp! — I have grown weaker, and I doubt if Leila herself could wake the old fuzzle for an hour or so. The flies were by this time a seething mass upon his manly master-member; they fed like coffin-worms at a lady's eyes. The sad soul stiffened; Captain Standish was himself again. This is an excellent method, explained the Archbishop; I have known it to succeed even in the direst extremity. When pross and prugge have done their dirtiest: when jill and jomer have given up the job: when Abbess and Artichoke have abandoned the article in derision: then has Beelzebub come to the rescue, and Father Abraham has believed the yarn about Isaac. Now, while I feel restored, I will ask you to accommodate me in your turd-trap, and I will sing you beautiful songs about the time when I was young. He was on my back before I could reply, and the fetid fuck-fritters of the foul-flip-flapped Father frizzled in my reeking rectum.

CAPITULUM VIII

NO! I SHALL not transcribe the songs the Archbishop sang. They were ill-suited to your dainty ears, my girls! No! In vain you strip your bellies and show me canoodles with gleet and pus a-dripping, and your dung-stuffed clyster-pipes choral in my ears and grateful to my smell. No, I say! I am adamant, iron! You may twist yourselves into the randiest positions you know; you may cuddle my crimson chitterling till it chirps, soars and spurts into the blue Heaven of God: but I will NOT corrupt your morals with those degrading and sinful songs. I will never transcribe a word or a syllable that the most modest woman need blush to hear: I will never be a party to the ruin of one innocent child-soul. Cunts! I protect you! Nugs! avaunt! Come not near the pure girls and women for whom I write this book, the decent sayings of a godly light of the Church. So let us gloss over the temporary lapse from politeness of the saintly old man — let us excuse one whose only fault was that he was born at a date when folk were less fastidious! — and let him return to the quiet and uneventful autobiography with which he has so far pleasantly and inoffensively regaled us.

Ah! You would, would you, you penny-a-peep flapper? Well, little girls will be little girls. Adam fell for less than this — Oh! if you suck so I shall go mad — Stop, for God's sake! This was the song.

THE ARCHBISHOP'S SONG

I nicked her suck-and-swallow,
   Her intercrural trench,
Her home-sweet-home, her hollow,
   Her little shop of stench.

I knocked her up the mustard-pot;
   I swivelled her in the socket;
I stirred her creamy custard-pot

With my rampageous rocket.

I jumbled up her harbour;
    I climbed her Jacob's ladder:
I slept inside her arbour;
    I stung her with my adder.

I larded her factotum
    I fucked her breadwinner;
My thrysus and its scrotum
    Gave her starch pie for dinner.

Her Mary-Jane I mashed,
    Her little sister jiggled;
Her sack of corn I thrashed ;
    Her horse-collar I niggled.

I stormed her Jack Straw's Castle;
    I jammed her tufted treasure;
I packed her paper parcel;
    I dug her mine of pleasure.

Her omnibus I boarded;
    I shagged her lover's locker;
Her Customs I defrauded:
    By Langolee! I block her.

I cleaned her saucy salmon;
    I piddled in her gutter;
I rubbed her greasy gammon;
    Her grotto I did futter.

I smoked her old red herring;
    I hogged her periwinkle;
I fulked her maiden erring:
    I watched her lower twinkle.

I went in to her tunnel;
    Put on Hans Carvel's ring;
Was filtered in her funnel,
    And goose-and-ducked her thing.

I split her rump, and vaulted
   The star above her garter;
Her strong-room I assaulted,
   And occupied her farter.

From which you all may gather
   That it will not be long
Before I am a father…
   And that is all my song.

There! let me alone now, and I will continue the Arch-bishop's recital.

How was it that days so sweet must pass? Oh Jimson! Oh divine maestro and thy Opera "Orange Pekoe"! To this hour the lust of thy dear shit-sewer sends the creamy essence of immortality all over my drawers. But it ended, and bitterly. The careless youth got too near S...y B.....s, and her breath killed him, as it would any creature higher in the scale of creation than a L..s or a H...s. They have the immunities of their crapulence. Broken-hearted, with a mentule like a weeping willow, save that it would not weep, I left the remains of my Stevie. Not without an effort to get even with the robber Death! I flung myself upon the dear corpse; I buggered him night and day, entirely surpassing— for I was now come to my strength — the childish efforts upon the queenly butter-boat of E.....d's debauched ruler. As the work of putrefaction proceeded — and the stench was awful, for S...y's little leaven had pervaded his whole lump — I rammed my arse-wedge frantically into his holes as they formed, as if in the insane hope of damming the damage of damned death's fell flood. Indeed for a week or so I did more than this. The patient actually gained weight. But time tells on the strongest. In the second week I kept barely level: in the third he steadily lost ground: in the fourth he fell to pieces under me: in the fifth I sedulously and conscientiously buggered the pieces one by one: but it was no good. Steven Jimson was (in the immortal word of Poe) a nearly liquid mass of loathsome, of detestable putrescence. Do not think for a moment that my affection was shaken by so slight a circumstance! But I assure you — nay! I swear it to you upon this holy Relic! (he produced a piece of the True Touch-her-home, with the Magdalen's clap-juice sticking to it still, and reverently kissed it) — that there was not one ounce of that body of love that could reasonably be firky-toodled any more. As long as anything that could be called Viscosity was inherent in the mass, I jounced it like a man. But this soon ceased: I reluctantly withdrew. Yet such was my love for my darling that I buggered a hole clean through his tombstone, and for six months I never left the hallowed spot. My spiritual superiors, however, soon put a spoke in my wheel. I should have been going on still, but they reminded me that I had a great career before me and that it was unworthy of a man — how much more of a Christian! — to allow a personal grief, however severe, to blind one for ever alike to the beauty and the duty of life. In vain I replied that there was now no beauty for me in the world, and that my duty was to my dead love. The Jesuit was subtle. To do this duty, he urged, you cannot remove this copper-stick of yours from the memorial stone. On the other hand I will assuredly cut it off if you do not so remove it, and that bloody quick! I don't want to wait here all day: I've a button-hole at home that needs my nosegay. Not so frigging fast, mister, if you please! I retorted: there are two sides to every argument. Cut it off, if you can! He instantly raised his sword, and directed a furious blow at the root of my aspersing-tool. The weapon broke. No! I am not boasting of the hardness of my tenant-in-tail: I would recall to your memory the scientific fact (see the researches of Herbert Jackson) that a jet of water, if but it be swift enough, is similarly impervious to mere steel. In all these months of constant buggery, without rest or respite, the rate of my tupping was practically unimpaired. But the greatest man is he who in the moment of victory imposes a reasonable condition of peace, not he who insults and drives to desperation an adversary perhaps ready to make a compromise mutually beneficial.

Come, father! I addressed the astonished priest. Let us be going: there are better turds in the arse than ever came out of it.

Such was my fond farewell to Stephen Jimson.

But Leila, who ran to embrace me, was for the first time in all her life defeated. For seven days she buffeted my beard-splitter like Palinurus and the waves; but she too failed. I had broken every record in the long-distance competition: and I needed rest. Even the pelvis of my boy love failed to rouse me: once the reaction had set in, nothing could stop it. On the eighth day Leila fell back with a weary and long-drawn howl: on the twenty-sixth she recovered sufficiently to try again: this time her efforts were crowned with success: a dribble of three drops of the precious fluid soaked into her mug, and tickled up the ulcers of her throat. I was again a man.

How inscrutable are the Ways of the Almighty! From those three drops came my three sons! Leila, her uvula irritated by the acrid fire of my extravagance, coughed it up and out. The three drops fell respectively upon the pouting bird's nests of three Nunnery hacks, who happened to be frigging themselves with no fear of the future! Nemesis overtook them! One and all conceived and bare sons and called their names Jesus, for they supposed that no man had been near them. Lost in the love trance, they had not suspected the insidious spermatazoa dropped as it were a ball upon the aphrodisiacal tennis courts of their Eden Gardens.

How I impregnated Leila herself, and the larks we had during her pregnancy, and the fun I had at her delivery — how different from the Monthly Drink, which I will also touch upon! — I will tell you when I have relieved my necessities — I am an old man of eighty now, and you must humour me — with the row of warm foetuses and pox-holes which my chaplain has just brought for my mid-morning performance.

CAPITULUM IX

The secret of Leila's affection for me, said the good old man, withdrawing his dripping jiggling-bone from a six months' kid spoilt by a sound, and inserting it in the still warm bowels of a still-born baby, was to be found in her fondness for the rapid and accurate repetition of the act of love. This I could supply, as you may imagine from my previous story; so we lived together in perfect harmony. Every month when her courses came on I revelled with peculiar lust in the miry bloodiness of her dearest bodily part. I would lie all day with her dumb-glutton perched on my aristocratic nose and chew the stringy mucus that issued smeary and glutinous from her bleeding privates: the taste I cannot hope to describe to you: you must taste it to appreciate it — ah! you sly dog! I see you have been there already — but it was beyond all praise. Hours flew by in this delightful occupation, she herself licking my beak with her enormous tongue (with which she could lick her nose) and playing over my cream cheeses with her fingers, while now and then her tongue would loose my love-dart and shoot up my brown and wrinkled stink-house, filling me with the most delicious sensations. For a change we would occasionally make the beast with two backs, and I would pump my mucky man-mess into her capacious milking-pail or not less accommodating manure-manufactory.

Sometimes I got a devil of a clap. My luckless claw-buttock would get twisted up with chordee till it resembled the horns of Ovis Poli rather than the mere picklock of a quiet and decent clerical gentleman. But the very stricture served its turn. The retention of semen in which lies the whole Art and Mystery of the brangle buttock game was much facilitated by the natural narrowing of the urethra: when I did come, it was more like an eruption of Mont-Pel'ee than a poor priest spunk-spitting at a meat-market. More, the acrid juice of the morbid secretion was far more exciting to the worn-out waste pipe of my gay Flirtina Cop-all than any mere baby-bouillon would have been. Her finish was more like that of a man in delirium tremens dying of strychnine poisoning, tetanus, and rattlesnake bites than a simple but merry-arsed Christian easing her yum-yum on a clergyman's sore throat.

With profound art she reserved her explosions till the supreme moment, and then, with one shriek hardly muffled by the tonsil-teaser in her mouldy mug, she would discharge her various secretions — vomit, frowsy towsy-mowsy fuck-muck, shit heralded by a Goetterdaemmerung of farts, and the rest, in an ecstatic touch-off, calculated to witch the world with noble arse-womanship; thereby obtaining that physiological relief which seems to our modern scientific philosophers the unnecessary excuse for the game of mumble peg.

The whole affair reminded one rather of a Crash of Worlds than of the usually less cosmic rootle of a gentle-woman's split mutton on the loose.

But not only in simple androgynation did she excel: she was great at flagellation: had she not been so, I should certainly have said she was, both out of respect for her — for what gentleman would care to dwell upon a flaw in an otherwise perfect character? — and because otherwise the English gentry would not buy your book, just as without the sodomy the English colony in Paris would be insensible to its charms.

Here, then, is a short account of an erotic scene of this character, in the most approved style of Mary Wilson.

To skate lightly over the preliminaries, there was a beautiful milliner, thought strict, but really very lascivious, and a little girl of twelve with a hairless crack complete, thought lascivious but really very strict: and her schoolmistress, a tall woman of thirty with an arse like a steam-roller, a coynte like a slate-quarry, and a clitoris like Lord Penrhyn, for it had been known to stand out for seven years against the demands of the workman. They got the little girl at a disadvantage over a chair, while Leila and I looked on with eyes injected with frightful lust at the voluptuous spectacle. The schoolmistress then addressed her little victim in these terms: "You saucy little bitch! you would, would you?" Excited to madness by the erotic phrase, she wildly lifted up her petticoats and exposed her magnificent rose. 'Twas a rooster that crowed like a hen that has laid an egg every time she thought of it, which happened about 67854 times a minute. She took a birch rod, and hit the little girl's b.t..m. What ho! What joy! "Yes!" she almost screamed, punctuating her remarks with violent blows, which — such was the height of her passion, as often as not missed the sufferer, who vainly pleaded for mercy, and promised never to do it again — "you slut! I will whip — whip — whip — whip — whip — whip — whip — whip — whip — whip— whip — whip — whip — whip — whip — whip — whip — whip — whip— whip — whip — whip — whip — whip — whip — whip — whip — whip— whip — whip — whip — whip — whip — whip — whip — whip — whip— whip — whip — whip — whip — whip — whip — whip — whip — whip — yes, whip — whip — whip whip whip whip whip whip whip whip whip whip whip whip whip whip whip whip whip whip whip whip whip whip whip whip whip whip whip whip whip whip whip whip whip whip whip you till the blood runs." Fatigued, she frigged herself and retired, leaving the now bleeding bum of the little girl to the milliner, who stuck a dildo up her shop and with the other hand wielded the dread instrument of torture. Oh! what a bum! she exclaimed: what a pleasure to beat it! What a dear bottom! I must — I will — can — I shall — I may, might, could, would, should, whip it. She had exhausted her auxiliary verbs and the auxiliary dildo (bought at the Auxiliary Stores) at the same moment, and the discarded godemiché dropped idle to the floor. Allow me, madam! said I, stepping forward for the first time. Thank you, father! she answered, and I insinuated my poperine pear into her fruit-basket. She then got down to business, and her birch flashed in the air.

> Above the girl, the birch-rod bright
> Was brandishing like gleam of light;
>   The arse was dark below;
> When with the ocean's mighty swing
> When heaving to the tempest's wing
>   She hit that open O: —

As Scott so narrowly escaped singing. Ah! she yelled, in a perfect transport of furious lust, I will whip — whip whip whip — whip whip — whip whip — whip — whip — whip — whip whip — whip — whip whip whip — whip whip — whip — whip whip whip whip — whip — whip whip — whip — whip whip whip — whip — whip whip whip whip whip whip — whip — whip whip — whip whip — whip — whip — whip — whip whip whip you, you darling. (Experts in flagellation are invited to notice the difference in metre between her and the fashionable schoolmistress.) This went on for such a long while the same that I think it will be better if you ask your readers to turn back to the beginning as often as they find necessary to produce the desired erection — on the principle of song music, and then finish as below, as it were at the close of the last verse.

The child was then unstrapped, and allowed to bathe her injured seat, while the fashionable schoolmistress and the fast milliner sat on a voluptuous sofa, and refreshed their flagging energies with wine and cake, talking over their past adventures and planning fresh scenes of lust and luxury.

But my own experiences were of a more serious sort. To my mind flagellation is a mere mockery if the victims survive it. I had attained my majority when my father resolved to give a great treat to celebrate it. His numerous negro slaves — yes, friend H..msw..th, I know you think I am lying, but my father, though living in France at the time of my birth, had subsequently bought a plantation in the West Indies, and I had dutifully gone out there for the joyful celebration — his numerous negro slaves — as I said before — oh yes, you are a clever fellow, I know slavery has been abolished in most of the West Indies, but my father lived on a secret island, which is not on the map, being protected from observation by the fogs produced by the incessant farting of its sea-faring population — his numerous negro slaves, — I hope everything is quite clear! — had been detected a little while before in a ramified and deep-seated conspiracy to shit outside the tubs of molasses, and thus rob their employer of the fruits of his careful system of dieting them on the refuse of the sugar-cane, and he was resolved to make their punishment an example to the whole island and at the same time to celebrate my majority in a manner befitting the auspicious occasion.

You will probably think it worth while to devote a whole chapter to this, and another to the pregnancy of Leila. I will therefore break off and put in an hour or so of tummy-tickling and twat-raking with some of the loose holes around, while you typograph the stuff you have got so far.

CAPITULUM X

Under the broad verandah of the family mansion the slaves were drawn up in line, and the overseers with long stock-whips and mighty stiff hair-splitters were guarding them and occasionally satisfying their lust upon the smoking arses of the negroes. My father and mother appeared with my sister and myself, and we lost no time in getting into position for those delights that are the cardinal of the family system all the world over. As it was my birthday, I had the chief place. My father's handsome quickening-peg burrowed my juicy bottom-hole, while my mother's central furrow was crushed upon my ploughshare as I lay on my back with my legs in the air. My sister squatted astride my head, and her cauliflower discharged its sweet sauce into my mouth. An ingenious arrangement of mirrors allowed us to see all that was going on, and at a sign from my father the head overseer brought forward a fattish young girl with a quite white skin. She yelled aloud for mercy, but it was no good. In a trice she found herself tied up to a triangle, and a lusty black was snipping great lumps out of her back with his whip. We raved in unison to her shrieks, and in one explosive foam of lust, jetted our family fountains at a single moment.

Before the woman fainted, the overseer gave the word to stop. She was a young and modest girl, and at his signal, three huge negroes bounded upon her. Heedless of her cries and tears they plunged their reeking arse openers into her dainty cat, into her shit-slot, and into her delicate mouth respectively. The last of the men was unlucky, for the teeth of the now agonizing girl scratched his treacle-tap, and hurt him. With a roar like a fiend the savage black, holding her by the hair, tore out her teeth by main force and again plunged his greasy gap-stopper into the talk-trap, thus partly drowning her pitiful cries, and nearly choking her when a second or two later his boiling bliss-blanc-mange foamed in a perfect cataract down her throat. At the same instant the twain at the lower end flooded her guts, not without breaking down the partition and turning the tender bowels of the luckless lassie into a sea of agony, for their acrid and poisonous slime corrupted whatever it touched. The girl was insensible. My father, furious at the sight, leapt up and struck her bleeding face again and again with his whip, but all in vain. They dissuaded him. When she comes to, he roared, fill her up with cayenne pepper and leave her in the sun! Another, a boy of ten years, was now brought up, and my mother, taking a needle and some fine silver wire, sewed up his urethra so tightly that no drop of liquid could possibly pass. She then took his young fiddlestick in her hand and by a thousand sensual touches awoke the lad's desire, while her own were attended to by a string of slaves whose fervid fornicators jobbed her tufted treasure. The agony of the poor boy grew terrible to behold: but the erotic fancy of my mother was unabated. In about an hour from the beginning something gave way in his inside; and in a dreadful shriek which my mother heard with a proud glad smile, kissing fondly the boyish lips, the blood gushed from his mouth, and he expired in torment.

It was now my sister's turn to choose the sport. Her lustful eyes fixed upon a fine and full-blooded negro, with a magnificent torso. Calling him up to her, she gave him a glance so fiery that the poor fellow was ravished. She slyly exposed her bonny Black Bess, and the man's nervous cane raised its beautiful head. She shrieked for help, crying that she was being raped by a slave. The overseer, who had assisted often enough at a similar pastime, raised his stick, and struck the offending pike-staff a severe blow, causing it to droop. The laughing girl continued her blandishments until the offence was repeated, and the punishment. Nearer and nearer she wove her delicious dances; again and again the cruel cane fell upon the Jack-in-the-Box of the now screaming slave: she came closer yet: with her fairy tongue she titillated the sensitive pudding, and sure as it ever rose, the overseer knocked it down with a sharp blow. This will teach you to cast your eyes upon your mistress, you dog! she raved at him, and pressed her hot and amorous beauty-spot against the bruised belly-ruffian. At last not even all her art could raise the drooping head: it was practically mashed into a pulp; her dainty mouth approached its bleeding tip, and with infinite lust she began to chew and swallow the entire intercrural pudding of the yelling black. She finished her meal by a savage bite at his hairy hangers, which she gulped down with every appearance of intense pleasure. Not content yet with the spectacle of anguish she had made, she then ordered his buttocks to be pierced with meat hooks, and pulled apart: this being done, she drove a wedge into his arsehole until the pelvis was completely broken. With a laugh of Hell, she wrote out his manumission, and gave it to him.

Her own passions were by this time at fever height. Nothing but a mule would do her, at the very least. Luckily, there was a stallion in the yard, and this beast was brought and put into position. Inch by inch he fought his way into her burning cave of harmony: and the lady between the extreme of rapture and agony, came again and again.

My own lusts were now to be considered. I decided upon a combination. One slave had his arse closely sewn up, and a dose of croton oil administered to him: another I smeared with sugar, and rolled in an ant-heap: a third I disemboweled and forced to feed upon his own steaming guts: a fourth and fifth — man and wife — I imprisoned, to be fed upon their own children, and after upon each other, mutilating them as far as possible without destroying life.

For my satisfaction, for the giving of these lascivious orders had all but turned my brain, I beheaded others, and plugged their windpipes with my rutilant ramrod, while the rest buggered me in turn. Not until night fell did I desist from the delightful sport, when my father exclaimed with a huge guffaw: By God's bollocks, Galahad, but there is nobody to cook the dinner!

But my sister was as clever as she was beautiful and good. The overseers gathered a fire of sticks, and she soon had some capital nigger meat broiling. For soup she gave us some stallion jelly from her chocked-up cuckoo's nest; for fish the scrapings of the old negresses' diddly-pouts made an excellent kedgeree: for entrée she did up a lot of balls, in shit sauce: also there was plenty of tripe, and some delicious sweetbread: for vegetables the stomachs of our victims were as good as a Covent Garden, for they lived exclusively upon the produce of the Earth: the relevé was a fine haunch. For sweets she passed round her own sweet strawberry-patch: and the savoury was no less easily procured from her luscious rectum.

She pissed white wine, spunked liquor, and gave us a better red than Burgundy: for by the greatest luck in the world, her monthlies had come on that very morning.

Ay! lad, we dined well.

Why should I dwell upon that night? Four in a bed, we drenched the sheets again and again. Not Leila herself could give me half the rapture I experienced from my sister and mother when they laid themselves out to give me a real good birthday, especially when my father, honest man! came to the rescue in his bluff hearty old English fashion. Ah!

CAPITULUM XI

It was a sad farewell when my career in the Church again dragged me from the arms of my reluctant family. Good-bye, sunny shores of the Hidden Island of the Caribbean Sea! Good-bye, delicious tirly-whirly of my lovely sister! Good-bye, incestuous ingle-nook of my mother, fiery flap-doodle of my manly sire! Never again perchance shall I see your dear faces: never again grope in your happy hunting-grounds for the game of grapple-my-belly.

With a heavy heart I set sail, and after a pleasant but uneventful voyage landed once more in England, to find that my little brochure on "Cunts; a few methods of fuckin' 'em" which had attracted the favourable notice of all classes, had been superseded by the lengthy and to my mind tedious monograph of a Turkish Mullah, entitled "Arseholes: some thoughts about suckin' 'em."

The table of my library (I was at this time vicar of Buckingham) was absolutely littered with appeals from the various dignitaries of the Church, including the Pope himself, urging me to devote my energies to preparing a counter-blast to the presumption of this audacious heretic. I complied. I issued a public challenge to him to compete with me on the floor of the Albert Hall, he to practice his dogma, and I mine. He refused, which was already something. When, next spring, I brought out my monumental Treatise on Heights and Hollows, embracing the entire subject, he again sank into deserved disesteem, and, vainly striving to restore his fallen fortunes with a poem on the culinary uses of placentas, which fell still-born from the press, gave up the unequal contest and had himself buggered to death in the principal Hamman of Constantinople.

The Pope signalized his approbation of my services by appointing me to a fat bishopric, with the run of all the choir-boys in the district. But I had my work cut out in other ways, for Leila was still with me, and you know from your own experience that she has but to grip once your father-confessor with her amazing man-trap, and it is not so easy to withdraw.

It fell on this wise. The English were still disembarking in interminable file upon the sunny shores of the Low Countries when my nine hundreth creamy emission for that period roared like the breaking of billows into that living fountain. We were wont to celebrate this emission, as its occurrence was wont to mark the near cessation of her tomato-jam season. Never for all my efforts had I managed to do the 1000. I fancy that 900 is somewhere near my physiological limit for one bout, as it were. On the best time I ever did, the figures were:

0-100,	83 min.	
101-200,	78 min.	
201-300,	57 min.	
301-400,	59 min.	
401-500,	68 min.	(Time lost on this heat by having to piss.)
501-600,	54 min.	
601-700,	60 min.	
701-800,	79 min.	
801-900,	93 min.	
901-1000,	266 min.	
1001-1100,	793 min.	

Abandoned in disgust.

You will wonder however how it was that Leila's monthlies did not last out the 1000, by the figures only 14 hrs, 57 min. The answer was that she was peculiarly constructed in this way. Her so-called "monthlies" occurred every four days, and lasted but twelve hours, never more. I was consequently biffed off every time about 925 or so.

The wisdom of this provision of Nature was soon evident.

The desirability of breeding another Leila had lent wings (to use a metaphor) to the reproductive mechanism of the lousy-notched barrack-hack. So that what follows will occasion no surprise in the truly scientific mind.

We celebrated the 900th creamy, as I said before, with a brief but glad hymn of praise to the God who had made us, and I withdrew my dripping bush-whacker for a moment in order to wipe it dry — nothing is so deleterious to the proper enjoyment of a game at Hey Gammer Cook as the too great slitheriness of the lady's rattle-bollocks — and in returning it to its sheath, the lassie was so pleased that she forgot for a second her role for protecting herself against danger of impregnation. This has always been to constrict the vagina in two places: near the vulva, to tighten on the master of ceremonies: and at the cervix, to prevent any of the fertilizing fluid, or, as she loved to call it, tool-treacle, from doing its deadly work. The remaining space, bigger than the Caves of Kentucky, was devoted to a cloak-room during the season, and to a universal shit-house for the wonderful collection of worms and other reptiles that she always loved to have about her. She had one tapeworm in particular — a fine fellow, I remember him well, he had an intellect like a Newton, and a tail like a toothpick — whom she dearly loved. So that there was no risk of harm happening. But on this occasion she let go, and my man-molasses, my posterity pudding if you prefer the phrase, soaked up into her womb, and she conceived and bare a host of children 36 days later. In vain I stood by her bedside, fucked them to death as they emerged, and threw them aside. I was beaten. I will not dwell upon this painful subject: suffice it to say that no less than 175 (all girls, with an admixture of monkey and slug from maternal impressions — infidelities I had long suspected without being able to prove) — were actually born and our reputations would have been ruined but for the cunning and resource which has ever brought me through the most difficult and adverse circumstances. I bribed the Pope's valet to conceal them in his Holiness' jerry-pot: when he perceived them, he supposed himself to be seized with a return of the Horrors, and gave orders for their instant destruction. When he learnt the trick that had been played on him, his anger was swallowed up in relief that it was not D.T. this time, and the humour of the thing striking him, he laughed and made me an Archbishop. Thus God can in his wonderful Workings bring good out of apparent evil.

I had wished to dwell for awhile upon the delightful memory of my Leila's fly-by-night as it appeared in the all too brief period of her pregnancy. Imagine the gradual heaving up of her greasy belly under one's very fuck, the constant tickling of one's thumb of love by the innumerable fingers new-made of the many foetuses, the curious slime that filled her, and floated one away into dreams of bliss not to be described! Yes, it was a glorious time — but, look here, young fellow, this talk is luring me away from my archiepiscopal duties. I have a meeting of bishops to bugger this afternoon: surely you have enough copy for a volume: I would suggest your slinging your hook and getting that chancre treated: I am sure you will say nothing about that unfortunate little contretemps of the Countess: and I hope to see you again sometime, and I will go on with the story of my life. Au revoir, then, and farewell! The Lord bless you, and keep you: the Lord lift up the light of his countenance upon you and give you peace: both now and for evermore, Amen!

He made the sign of the Cross, spat in my left eye, and spunked in my right; then ushered me to the door with courtly politeness. At the gate he impressed a loving kiss upon my arsehole, and gave a final but business-like frig to my weary yard.

I passed out: the great Churchman was but a memory in my life.

JUVENILIA

THE NEEDS OF THE NAVY

The air of the room was quite sweet and heavy with the savour of forbidden kisses; a faint moist sense of sweat steamed up in the twilight, and there was a sound of breath that did not dare to breathe, of sighs choked by fear. The midshipman's head silently turned round and his tongue pushed languidly forward to touch the lips of the lieutenant. A sound in the next room; both trembled violently, sprang from the sofa where they had been lying and hastily arranged the disorder their passion had made necessary. The middy took his lover's hand, raised it to his lips, bit it hard with sudden mad desire and whispered, in a voice shuddering with unsatiated lust "Ah God! Ah God! I love you now!" He slipped through the door and left Andrew Clayton to sweet memories and disquieting thought of the future. For Monty Le W... had never given him his love before. Monty was a dark, languid-eyed boy with jetty hair; there was about him the indefinable air that sexual perverts recognize so quickly, a closer union than masonry can boast. In fact, he had not been on board H.M.S. Osiris a week before the Captain had promoted him to a dignity sufficiently high to excite the envy of the boys who had till then held the proud distinction of favourite catamite. A furious battle between the jealous beauties ended in their growing so excited over the spilt blood and the violent physical pain that the spectators were scandalized by the sight of an impromptu orgie as infuriate as the fight had originally been. The boys were still fast friends, but Monty was first favourite with the Captain and tyrannized over him to the previously-unheard-of extent of demanding reciprocity en affaire d'amour. The Captain on his part only asked fidelity; and indeed Monty had grown to love him so dearly that the thought of an adultery would have been insupportable. One day, however, a sudden desire came upon him towards the most popular of the lieutenants,

Andrew Clayton, a man of violent passions not usually associated with fair hair and rather timid grey eyes. Andrew saw the sly looks of the midshipman and one day went into his cabin and, stepping to his side without a word, gave him a fierce kiss, while his hand sought to awake desire in an even more direct manner. But the passing fancy of the boy had gone, and he rudely repulsed the advances of his would-be lover. Andrew, with great self-command, withdrew in silence. Next day, however, they were both called before the Captain, read a long lecture on the sin of paederasty and severely reprimanded. It was evident that Captain Spelton liked his forehead very well as it was, and meant to keep a sharp look-out. Monty in his innocence was terribly indignant and naturally became quite ready to cuckold the Captain if he could. At mess that evening he managed to whisper "you shall have me if you still — " the immediate result of which was considerably embarrassing to Andrew. But all the endeavours they made to meet and steal a kiss occasionally were always frustrated as if by accident, though they now knew it must be of set purpose. Andrew suggested at last that, to allay suspicion, he should choose another middy and pretend to make violent love to him. Monty's jealousy said no, and only after a long time was he persuaded to agree. "Katie" Ambrose, the boy selected for this vicarious duty, was a dirty little fellow of the most vicious type. His favourite fancy, in public, was to lie on his back and to endeavour to catch in his mouth, and swallow, his own emissions, and he was also constantly degrading his rank by licking the genitals, or the feet, of the dirtiest sailors and stokers on the ship. He was only glad from the social status it gave him when Andrew made overtures of love. Monty would have himself preferred this choice, arguing that Andrew would have himself preferred this choice, arguing that Andrew could never be really enamoured of so vicious a boy, but what he saw three weeks after undeceived him. On this wise.

One night the Captain, being restless, suggested a tour of

inspection, and the two lovers stole quietly out of their cabin. They came after a time to where Andrew and Ambrose were, and were lucky enough to catch the former in the very act of sacrificing at the most holy altar, while the boy, turned half round, was gently chewing and licking the armpit of the perspiring lieutenant. One finger of his free hand sought to penetrate the other's shrine, while the hand underneath him titillated his own genitals in unison with the motions of his lover. The act was consummated; gasping, heaving, breathless, they sink lower on the bed. Their tongues mingle lazily; the elder man withdraws slowly; a pleasant sound announces his exit. Hardly a moment and the boy gives his lover a signal. The latter turns over while Ambrose rises and sits over him while the sweet salt offering, spiced now by the god to whom it is offered, trickles daintily into the open mouth of the languorous man. Then the boy slips down into his lover's arms: they share the incense with mingled mouths until the flavour is appeased and they swallow it with the first blush of reawakening desire. "Katie" eagerly reverses his position to prepare for a new embrace; but Monty whispers to the Captain: "Darling, I can bear it no longer; come back!" They never slept at all that night; but I never heard either of them regret the fact. But Monty was terribly disgusted with Andrew, and when little Ambrose struck Monty (who had called him, with naive eloquence, "Suck-shit") the latter knocked him down and kicked him. The lieutenant, who was near, had to interfere, and the dark languorous boy was punished. This mean revenge (as he understood it) irritated Monty still more and he eventually refused to speak to Andrew at all.

It was the night of a big dinner ashore and Monty Le W... had gone up to a little sitting-room which was next to the billiard-room, to wait for the Captain. Unperceived Andrew had followed him and was now lurking behind the heavy curtain that hung over the door; he listened to the boys' muttered soliloquy, disturbed only by the noisier laughter and curses of the billiard-room. Spelton was long-damned long-coming; no doubt of that. And Monty's desires were getting less controllable every minute. At last he took down his trousers and began to play with himself, hoping to ease a little his discomfort. At this moment Andrew glided forward and whispered "If you speak we are both lost. Your dress…" The frightened boy made a movement of agony. He was terribly angry, and yet dared not speak or make the least sound. After the other affair he knew the Captain would never believe his story. The lusty lieutenant took out a weapon fiery and enormous, and began to seek admission. The boy, with all the force of the sphincter, resisted. A sharp tap or two on the coccyx, however, reminded him that he had a bold lover, who would stick at nothing, and he gave way. The whole length of his lover's yard was engulfed in one great push, and, accustomed as he was to the Captain's penis, he could hardly repress a cry of pain. The ravisher was far longer and thicker and cared a great deal less about any pain he might inflict. And he plunged like a mad horse! At last the welcome climax, and a perfect deluge of kisses bitten hard into his olive neck. And then the luxurious confession with which this story began.

Left to himself, Clayton invented incidentally twenty-three quite new curses, called Le W… a little bitch, kissed the mark of the little bitch's teeth on his hand, and generally conducted himself as an officer and a gentleman would do, provided he were also a devout Christian. He foresaw trouble. It came pretty quickly. Two days afterwards Clayton had to quit his lover's room in a great hurry, as heavy footsteps trod the passage. The Captain was in his dressing-gown and proved quite Arcadian beneath. He was in bed in a jiffy, and discovered heat and moisture to an extent unwarranted by the climate. "I thought you would never come, love," sighed the charming middy, with resourceful tact, "so I've been whiling away the time." "I'm here now," said his lover, and applied his lips to the dark altar of his desire. That was very moist too, and the Captain's inquisitive tongue soon penetrated its secrecies and became aware of a strong warm taste as of incense recently offered. "I envy you your amusement," he observed, with delicate irony, "you appear to have succeeded at last in following my advice to go and bugger yourself!" He said no more just then, but came round with a sharp knife two days later to both the lovers and said he thought their accomplishments, if unique, were unnatural. But the knife cut both knots at once; he told Lord Cartington at their tête-à-tête dinner the next day that there seemed to be no end to the variety of entrees which had as a basis — oysters.

"Katie" Ambrose grew in wisdom and stature and in favour with god and man.

AFTER THE FALL

A Page from the Book of the Recording Angel

Adam had gone down to the Euphrates for a morning's sport with the Icthyosaurus. The day before he had no luck at all with a rather big fly (pterodactyl-wing and angel-hackle) and meant to spin with the artificial dodo for a bit before giving up the water as hopelessly over-fished. He had better have stayed home, though, and kept a sharp look-out with the gaff for the serpent. This is what happened in his absence.

Eve had done her day's work, and was sprawling in the sun with her tailor-made fur-lined dress within easy reach (fig-leaves, in the daytime, had entirely gone out, and were now only worn for evening dress), and meditating on the curious events of the past evening. "Silly thing that of Adam's," she soliloquized, "just when I was feeling nice, it turned sick and collapsed, and took ten minutes to get well again. Why, I could have gone on all night without those silly intervals! And the old fool says it tires him and he can't dig today because his back aches, so he's gone fishing. Fishing! I'll fish him when he comes home. I believe he's gone to see that lioness he was so fond of in the old days. She was rude enough to both of us yesterday though — so are all the beasts since we ate that apple Lord God made all the fuss about. The serpent's as much a gentleman as ever, of course. He was at the same public school as Lord God, he says. I'm sure he's got better manners, though! The old wretch! To tell me about travail and labour and that rubbish-besides, a really nice God would keep his smoking-room jokes to himself another time. And the brute never made love either. I'll be even with him one day. I do wish this hole wouldn't itch. Rubbing's no good-oh! It's better when I rub hard. There! It's started again now I've left off. I'll rub harder this time. Ah! Adam! Adam! — Ha! I thought I was with Adam — Oh, how lovely!" And she gave a delicious little sigh.

"Pardon this intrusion, Duchess, pray" said a new voice, in the well-bred deferential manner that is so characteristic of diplomats. "But is it the third Wednesday, is it not?"

"My dear Prince, how good of you to come. I was just hoping some one would drop in and cheer me up. This move has left me quite a wreck."

"Ah! Duchess, you are more beautiful than ever."

"Bad man — "

"Yes, and deserve a better husband."

"Adam is as good as — "

"But his poor health. He's had a cold ever since he left Eden, this climate is so terribly uncertain."

"Yes, he's not very strong, poor man."

"He gets tired easily."

"Yes" with a sigh.

"I see you have been doing your best to supply his place." For Eve had not changed her position during this interview, and her moist fingers still played among the golden hair.

"Oh! I didn't mean to."

"Ah! Duchess, what a pity — and what a surprise!"

"Yes, it did feel like it. But really, Prince, you're as inquisitive as that rude old Lord God."

"You are not offended with me?"

"How could I be? How ever shall I repay you for giving me that wrinkle about the apple?"

"I must really apologise for being indirectly the cause of that old curmudgeon's insolence."

"Not a word. I am all gratitude."

"Only half gratitude, Duchess."

"?"

"Because you have only half the secret."

"And the other half is?"

"Naughty."

"You darling, tell me at once."

"Will you kiss me?"

"Kiss you — come here — Satan!"

"Eve!"

And his lithe coils rolled over her naked body, his forked tongue slipped beneath the white teeth and its delicate foam maddened her tongue. It touched her tender palate, and withdrew to penetrate her dainty nostrils. All round her he wrapped his soft green folds and their gentle pressure warmed her blood that shuddered with love to feel him, cold and slimy, embrace her bosom and her lissom thighs. Always his tail penetrated her half-opened fountain and gently tickled the rosy tongue of love, that now grew swollen and stiff with excitement. Eve broke into a hot, foul sweat. "Satan! I love you! When Adam kisses me he is so hot and heavy; he chokes me! You lift me, you hold me, you — Ah!" The tail gave a determined push, and the perspiring woman gasped with pleasure. "My Queen!" "Satan!" The amorous snake withdrew his coils from her breast. "Don't you love me?" "I will teach you a love your Adam does not dream of!" And his head sought the dark home of her desire, while he pressed in her red lips the most tender part of his eager body. She entered into his desires and abandoned herself to the new vice with rapture. Again and again she deluged him with love-drops, and the warm odour of their bodies went up, a delicious steam, till his head withdrew, foaming, and fell upon her reeking lips again to lick salacious kisses and gently chew her gentle eyelids when she turned her mouth again to an even dearer object.

Suddenly a shout was heard far off, and, rising up, Satan saw Adam returning with the spoil. He was now too near for him to escape. Eve with quick woman's wit gathered her furs to her and squatting in front of the wood fire forced herself to appear nonchalant, while Satan gathered his coils together under her skirts. The fire blazed up as she tended it, and Adam joyfully saluted his mate with the patronizing air a man always thinks it proper to adopt with a social, physical and intellectual inferior. She received it with all the docility which an unfaithful woman is careful to assume. But she was by no means as easy as her countenance would have indicated. Her serpent-lover was taking a mean advantage of her confusion to attack her in two places at once — her worn-out passions were being frightfully stimulated, and she did not think she could possibly maintain her balance at the supreme moment. And Satan was really venturing terribly far. Up and up he writhed, and the mouth of her womb spasmodically closed and re-opened in vain. He penetrated more and more deeply, and at last, with a convulsive wriggle, disappeared entirely into the temple of love at the very moment Eve, in a strong shudder, consummated her suppressed desire and fell to the ground in a swoon. Adam was alarmed. Some burnt clippings of mastodon-hoof were effectual in restoring her, but Eve's furs had fallen off again, and Adam divined the nature of his good lady's excitement. "To think now," he observed, with pardonable pride, "that the mere sight of me — or would it be the smell? I'll write a book about it and try to make up my mind that way. Poor girl! I know it won't be fit for work tonight. The lioness used to lick it with some effect, I remember. Couldn't ask Eve to do that, though. It would degrade her, I'm sure. I must try and raise her to my level rather than — Damn that potato patch! It must be dug over tomorrow, and only the old flint spade still. A man in Lord God's position — House of Lords, stake in the country, and all that — ought to provide iron spades — this is the only country planet for billions of miles where science hasn't penetrated, so that young prince says — don't believe he's a real prince, though — took all that cursing from a simple Lord like a lamb — says it's beneath his dignity to swear back. I'd have had the bugger up for criminal libel. Threatened him, too, about Eve's baby smashing his head." But at this point a prowling megatherium wailed and Adam snatched up a sling and started off to drive him away. Eve lost no time in knocking violently on her belly. "Time to get up, sir. I'll bring your hot water in a minute!" Satan awoke, and not being fond of water, hot or otherwise, unless with a considerable portion of Mammon's old Highland Hell-fire, climbed down, put his head out, and asked what the devil the knocking was about. "Get away, dear, Adam's gone out for an hour, quick, and don't hurt me." "No, Eve, I will spend the night with you." "But Adam?" "Let him come in too." "No, he'll discover everything. I'd rather any other plan." "My plan is necessary — you don't know all the secret yet." And with an affectionate little snap at the clitoris as he passed, Satan again withdrew into his cosy hiding-place.

Adam soon returned victorious from his raid, and was very glad to lay his fur aside, and seek the embraces of his consort. Any doubts he might have had were soon removed by Eve whose mass of tawny hair soon hung over his thighs, while her little red mouth proceeded to excite him to the proper degree of rigidity. It was soon obtained, and she quickly changed her position to bestride him, while her hand guided him to the proper orifice. The dance began. Eve wriggled her fat bottom about as hard as she could, and Adam assisted as far as his constrained position would allow. The critical moment arrived and a deluge of warm liquids mingled to flood the surrounding parts. But Eve would not let him withdraw as yet. And at this moment Adam gave vent to a cry of pain. "I'm bitten," he said. "That horrible Palaeopulex," said Eve. "No, it's in you! It's pushing me out! Get up!" And Eve jumped up alarmed to find Satan quietly emerging from his citadel. Adam jumped for a club. But by the time he arrived a change had arisen. The old snake-skin dropped and Satan stood in his own shape, a radiant spirit. "You bit me," said Adam, embarrassed. "For your own good! God doomed you to death. My bite has filled your blood with a poison that will take away Death's terrors, that will make him welcome even!" "What is this poison called?" said Eve. And Satan replied "Syphilis!" As he went away he laughed. God did not like to hear him.

THE PARSON'S PRAYER

There was a priest who took much pleasure
    In amorous discourse o'night.
His only sorrow — that a measure
    Was placed unto his might.
He prayed — let not his words escape us! —
    Unto Priapus.

"Thou God whom constantly I serve
    (As constantly as any can)
Endow me with more strenuous nerve,
    Make me a mightier man!
Increase my powers of ejection!
    Grant me more erection!"

The god took heed unto his prayer —
    A faithful servant deserves pay —
Yet, pondering, fingers run through hair,
    He curtly answered "Nay"
His suppliant, wrathful, then departed
    Half broken-hearted.

But Mercury had chanced to listen
    While these remarks were being made.
His mischief-loving eyeballs glisten.
    He touched the man, and said:
"Priapus is an old curmudgeon !
    Go not in dudgeon!"

"I will accede. Be henceforth gifted
    With everlasting power to stand
Without a maiden's finger lifted
    Or touches from a harlot's hand.
No trusty tongue shall waste your money;
    Nor sight of cunnie."

The man rejoicing, went his way
    Exclaiming "Thanks beyond expression"
He sought the Strand, and, sooth to say,
    Began to try his new possession.
So, picking up a hoary harlot
    Who blushed quite scarlet

At such immodest words addressed to her,
    Yet did not blush to ask five pounds,
He took her home, and there confessed to her
    His admiration knew no bounds.
And she agreed (vide the sequel)
    His power was equal.

All night he kept his engine going
    Much to the lady's satisfaction,
Till in the morning, by her showing,
    His total (after due subtraction
Of income tax) was found in fine
Eleven thousand and eighty nine!

Still, as through years the solid rocks stand,
    No weakness did this hero show.
He still possessed a mighty cock stand
    When his fair mistress had to go,
And he repaired to wash his balls
Before he paid his social calls.

But — Nemesis! — The drawing-room
    Is not the place for exhibition
Of that which satisfies the womb.
    At last involuntary emission
Relieved him with such sudden glee
As to upset his cup of tea.

Also he found inconvenient
    When urchins shouted "Good old stand!"

When at a dance, the matrons lenient
    Would cough and smile behind a hand.
And maidens with gazelle-like eyes
Observe with wondering surprise.

Besides, an everlasting aching
    Kept him for ever on the shove
At lunch or tea, asleep or waking,
    He felt the gentle hints of love.
A parson too (O who could doubt it?)
    Is best without it.

When he began to read the text
    Preparatory to his sermon
'Twould rise, and he, beginning vexed,
    Would end by sundry oaths in German,
Whose tendency to edification
Was not clear to his congregation.

By day, by night, eternal stands!
    One long continuous emission —
He left his cure in other hands
    And sought his cure of a physician,
Who marvelled at his tale of tooling
As at a pretty piece of fooling.

But, soon convinced, he diagnosed
    This case as clearly as could be;
"You suffer, sir (no, be composed!)
    From a mistaken chastity.
Indulge your natural desires
And quench those fires!"

That man he smiled; and bade him mark
    A large blue paper signed and checked
By Turquand, Bishop, Young and Clarke,
    As "audited and found correct"

Which said "accomplished in a month
The seventeen million and sixty oneth!"

They tried low diet, circumcision,
    Injection, medicine, inhalation,
They tried a vain hypnotic vision,
    They tried cold water and castration,
In vain — the tool persistent stood it all;
Doctor and surgeon did no mortal good at all.

The patient died. His coffin crowned with flowers
    From various ladies — roses, lilies, laurel,
As some last tribute to his wondrous powers
    Was oak, and bound with brass. The moral
Of this sad tale is so extremely patent
That to repeat it were banal and blatant.

Learn from this fable — counterfeit presentment
    (Shakespeare) Of Truth — this fact (I've sought
        it far!)
The best of blessings is divine contentment,
    (Shakespeare again) and in particular
(Seek not to exceed in matters of virility
God-given ability!)

THE BROMO BOOK

PARODIES

LONG BEFORE DAWN

Sweet cunt, if prick were stronger,
Arse clear of turds that wrong her,
Then two things might live longer
    Two sweeter things than they.
J.T. the root of power,
And balls, the bloomless bower.
J.T. that stands an hour,
    And balls that droop a day.

From entry to emission
When passion melt suspicion,
The pot is there to pish on,
    The paper is there for turds,
As fart by fart grows colder,
And shit on brows or shoulder
Slides sideways now, and smoulder
    The lusts too sweet for words.

This one thing once worth poking
God gave (alas! in joking)
The cunt that needs no stoking.
    The prick that always stands
Were mate most fit to find her
(Were any luck) to grind her,
And then slip in behind her
    While frigging fast with hands.

Ah! one cunt worth the tickling,
One stream of spunk worth trickling!
Ah sweet! one prick worth pickling
    In such a slimy still!
To frig you till one chilled you;
To damp you till you mildew:

To fuck you till one filled you,
    Sweet cunt, if spunk could fill:—

To hunt a crab and lose him
Between your twat and bosom,
Your bubbies' coppery blossom,
    Between your hips and hocks:
To say of clap "What is it?"
To laugh at syphilis, it
Is nothing; we can kiss it
    And it's no longer pox:—

To feel the buboes thicken
By ulcer-blooms that quicken,
Red sores that stink and sicken,
    Lures of a leprous bride:—
Till, like a luscious Turk, you re-
Bound, to the doctor spur: cure he
Will, quickly blending Mercury
    With Kalic Iodide.

(A verse, too indelicate for the taste of our lady
readers, has here been omitted.)

As when late larks give warning
Of dying fucks or dawning,
Girls murmur in the morning:
    "Once more, dear boy, once more!"
And Mr. Pego failing
To answer to her wailing,
Bursts out in wrath and railing:
    "I shan't, you bloody whore!"

But soon her mouth up swallows
His prick; her poxy hollows
Grow glorious as Apollo's:
She shoves it up her bumb,

Those buttocks fat dividing.
Ah! Soon his head is hiding:
For love hath no abiding,
 But dies before the come;

So hath it been, so be it!
Get out of bed and pe! It
Is time the doctor see it,
 Or smell it: — care I which?
Lest all who loved and licked your
Fat oyster get a stricture:
For though you are a picture,
 You are a rotten bitch.

RONDEL

Kissing her twat, I sat between her feet,
Smelt it, and felt it: sucked and found it sweet:
Made fast her legs, drew down her clitoris
Long as long pricks, and juicy like a kiss
With her own fingers played upon the spot
    Kissing her twat.
Shit were no sweeter than her spend to me!
Shit of dead lobsters under the cold sea!
What fart could get between my lips and hers?
What new sweet splutter of her hairy arse?
Unless perhaps her spitting piss me shot,
    Kissing her twat.

ODE TO TITE

(Fragment)

When the harlot refuses the oyster,
    And the pandar is left in the lurch;
When the cunt is discrowned of the cloister,
    And the choir boy unkissed of the church;
When Aum tat Savitur varenyam
    The Hindu forgets to recite,
We should think we had reached the millennium,
    Save only for Tite!

STEPHANOS

With songs from the Isis o'erladen
    Thou stand'st in the battles full
Disdaining the breast of the maiden
    And spurning her fatuous cunt.
Brave buggery's fervent apostle!
    We fuck thee until we are faint,
Our comrade of cockstands colossal,
    O, Stephane, saint!

Nor wall-hole nor girl-hole no grass-hole
    Accepts thy implacable cock;
But the brown, wrinkled crease of an arse-hole
    Is thine for — the furious block;
When fervent and swollen the torrent
    Of solid and spasmical spend
Rolls luminous up through the horrent
    Back-side of a friend!

Thou hast come, and the great anticlimax
    Is pallid in face of the dawn;
But thy joy with a quickmoving eye Max
    B..rb..m has rapidly drawn.
A penis erect is thy totem,
    Thy fetish a boot — very quaint!
But thy visage resembles a bottom,
    O, Stephane, saint!

The garlands that crowned you and girt you,
    Of feminine: figures and frail
Are torn from the bosom of virtue
    By sodomy's gustier gale.
For the songs that you lured us to love with
    Are chains of a decadent art;
And the chants that availed us to shove with
    Are those of a fart.

O legs like the legs of the Saviour!
    O feet! O, immutable toes!
O mute and impressive behaviour
    Of thy stallion aquiline nose!
O eyes not of lust but of languor!
    O lips not of flesh but of paint!
Bite hard, though of course not in anger,
    O, Stephane, saint!

When the stars of the heaven are bust up,
    And the earth tails away from the sun;
Thou wilt still be as ready to thrust up
    Thy penis, till penes are done:
And the boys that come northward from Naples
    Together shall cling and to thee.
If ye cannot ape heaven ye can ape hells.
    And so can the sea.

O foolish and hideous hucksters
    That linger by bubbie and quim!
Your days are ridiculous fucksters
    Are drawn into twilight, and dim.
For in spite of the Virgin her limp son
    We are tinged with the sodomite's taint:
All owing to thee, Mr Jimson,
    O, Stephane, Saint!

A SNATCH

If clap were what the babe is
And pox were like the cot.
Our things would rub together;
We'd roger hell for leather
Despite of gleet and tabes,
Grey penis or green twat;
If clap were what the babe is
And pox were like the cot.

If I were what the turds are
And love were like the arse.
With double sound and single
Delight our farts would mingle,
With music filled as birds are
That walk about the grass;
If I were what the turds are
And love were like the arse!

If you were crabs, my darling,
And I your love a taenia;
We'd scratch and strain together
My rubber and your leather
Until we both were crazy
(My stage and your proscenia)
If you were crabs, my darling.
And I your love a taenia.

If you were thrall to chancre
And I were page to piles.
We'd play for boric acid
Until we grew more placid.
Assuaged our native rancour
And broad our mouths with smiles:
If you were thrall to chancre
And I were page to piles!

If you were fucking's lady
And I were lord of buggery,
We'd work electric handles
To dildos, sticks, and candles.
Till testicles kept hey-day
In vulvas greasy snuggery:
If you were fucking's lady
And I were lord of buggery.

If you were queen of spending
And I were lord of spunk,
We'd fuck for days together
And oil your chamois-leather,
And teach my tool a bending.
And prove your twat a skunk,
If you were the queen of spending
And I were lord of spunk.

EPILOGUE

If I were bubo's victim
And you orchitis' prey
We find what strange delight is
In epididymitis.
Your cock — the tongues that licked him
Would have the deuce to pay
If I were bubo's victim
And you orchitis' prey.

TO PE OR NOT TO PE

KING.

O heavy burden!

POLONIUS.

Hold on, I'm coming: I'll withdraw, my lord
                    [*Enter Hamlet.*]

HAMLET.

To pe or not to pe: that is the question:
Whether 'tis nobler in the mind to suffer
The slings and arrows of outrageous stricture
Or to take arms against a closed urethra
And by abscission, end it? To fuck: to come:
No more; and, by a come to say we end
The cockstand and the thousand natural lusts
That flesh is heir to. 'Tis a consummation
Devoutly to be wished. To fuck: to come:
To come, perchance to clap! Ay, there's the rub.
For from that come of fuck what clap may catch
When we have shuffled off this mortal stand
Must give us pause. There's the chordee
That makes calamity of so wet dreams!
For who would bear the jerks and drops of piss,
The piss pot's wrong, the bladders contumely,
The pangs of prostate gland, the pe's delay,
The insolence of orchids, and the spurns
That patient merit of the urethra takes
When he himself might his quietus make
With a greased catheter. Who would sandal swill
To fart and shit under a potent purge
But that the dread of something after gleet.
The senile stricture from whose imminence

No catheter gives 'scape, puzzles the will,
And makes us rather bear the ills we have
Than fly to others that we know not of.
Thus chordee doth make cowards of us all!
And thus the native need of urination
Is sicklied o'er with the pale cast of thought
And enterprises of great piss and po, meant
With this regard, their currents corkscrew turn
And lose the name of pumpship. Soft you now!
The fair Ophelia! Nymph, in thy orisons
Be all my sins remembered.

OPHELIA.

Good my lord,
How does your honour for this many a day?

HAM.

I humbly thank you! Well, well, well.

OPH.

My lord, I have remembrances of yours
That I have longed to redeliver:
I pray you now receive them.

HAM.

No, not I.
I never gave you aught.

OPH.

My honoured lord, you know right well you did.
[*Left disputing.*]

ALL THE WORLD'S A BROTHEL

All the world's a brothel,
And all the men and women whores and buggers.
They have their exits and their entrances.
And one man in his time lets many farts.
His arsehole being an octave. First the Infant
Violently rogered by an aged duke:
And then the frigging schoolboy, with his scrotum
And shining gland, his spend mere slime of snail
Unwilling from the tool. And then the lover
Fucking like a furnace, with a woeful ballad
Made to his mistress' bottom. Then a soldier
Full of stiff spunk and bollocked like the bull,
Jealous of sapphists, sudden and quick to come,
Seeking the bubble gonorrhea
Even in the bitch s mouth. And then the justice
In fair round belly soaked with mercury
With stand severe, and fuck of formal type,
Full of wise tricks and modern aids to love;
And so he lets his fart. The sixth age shifts
Into the lean and slippered pantaloon
With drooping penis, balls withdrawn in belly,
His youthful whore well fucked, a world too wide
For his shrunk prick: and his big manly piss,
Turning again toward childish treble, pipes
And whistles in his sound. Last scene of all
That ends this strange eventful history
Is second impotence and mere castration:—
Sans prick, sans balls, sans stand, sans everything.

HOME THOUGHTS, FROM ABROAD

O to be in Clara,
Now her monthly's there!
And whoever spends in Clara,
Finds some morning unaware
That the tip of his prick in its brushwood nest
Is red and inflamed and — you guess the rest!
At least he is sorry he sped the plough
    In Clara — now.

And after chordee, when gleet follows,
And zinc he injects and santal swallows!
Hark, where his twisted love-plant pees in jerks
The mucus-laden urine of the lover,
Wakes the gross hufflahs, scares the scampering
    quirks!
That's the small stricture, makes you piss twice
    over
Lest you mistake for an unequalled scorcher
The first fine careless torture!
Yet. Though his outlook's rough, his whore is due.
All will be gay when sucking wakes anew
The bollocks, every lousy bitch's dower.
Far creamier than this gaudy dildo-shower!

ONE WAY OF LOVE

I

All June I rubbed my prick with grease.
Now, hair by hair, I comb its fleece,
And shew it where Pauline may pass.
She will not suck me off.
Alas! What, no luck? Lord love a duck!
The chance was she might need a fuck!

II

How many months I strove to wipe
My brown and corrugated pipe!
To-day I fart for all I know.
She will not hear my music. So?
It is split? Devil a bit!
Suppose Pauline had bade me shit!

III

My whole life long I learned to frig.
This hour I play the supreme pig
And suck her pussy. Pox or clap?
She will riot give me syph? Mayhap!
Pox who may — I still can say
"Those who get chancre, lucky they!"

OUTSIDE THE SPANISH CLOISTER

(ODE TO A.W.P. ESQ.)

Foetus-face! I hate your swinish
 Snivels against what is good.
Mixed with pseudo-libertinish
 Would-be-naughty-if-you-could
Show of dirty words from drabs
 Picked up east of Leicester Square.
Yes! The Ocean hath its crabs.
 (Otherwise? Bah! God knows where.)

Climb the Matterhorn — with porters
 To pretend you need no guide!
You — O God! — seduce the daughters
 That smile smugly at your side.
You the debauchee of — Zermatt!!
 You! Who cannot see a snub.
Skin-thick! Skull-thick! παχυς δερματος
 Off, Lilith! There's the rub.

Teach your engineers to bore!
 (There your teaching none should lack.)
Medicine's rotten to the core.
 Slap the doctor on the back!
Tell the trainer and the jockey
 How to win a coming race!
Tell the geologist how rocky
 They are. (Joke!) You foetus-face!

Shakespeare said — O you say better
 Much — Bah! Shakespeare was a stoat!
Damn the spirit! Damn the letter!
 Would to God I had your throat
Blackening in my fists! You humbug!
 Grovel, or I'll smash your head.

Legacy? You'll leave me some bug
    (Won't you, foetus?) When you're dead.

Ugh! I hate to prate as much as
    (Magpie, marker!) I hate you.
Let me once get such a clutch as
    (Rhymes — that's one and one — that's two!)
David got on Jacob — was it?
    Muddleheaded, eh? Perhaps
I've no cellular deposit
    In my mind like Cambridge chaps.

Swine and snob! I hate your snotty
    Snarls — to heel, you mongrel! — Steeth!
Once I ripped — εχτεινα ποτε
    Such another from beneath.
You, you festering reptile! Shelley
    Would have — I forget the place —
Damn the place! Up, Guards! Impelle
    Hastam! Smash you! Foetus-face!

FRAGMENT

PARODY ON THE HYMN
"THERE IS ONE ABOVE ALL OTHERS"

Rose, your fuck is simply ripping.
    (O how he loves!)
How your cunt my prick is gripping!
    (O how he loves!)
In and out its head is slipping,
Filling you with joy, and whipping
All your cream to mutton dripping!
    (O how he loves!)

FORCE

Jim Dumps was down upon his luck
Because he could no longer write a smart article on the
fiscal question.

He used to growl and groan and grunt
Because he could not ease a sub-editor's mind when the
paper was a column short and only an hour to press-time.

Force so renewed his vital powers
That he could keep it up for hours;
And now he wallows in a bluebook
The people call him Sunny Jim.

LIMERICKS

I

There was an old man of Manchuria,
Who suffered from painful dysuria,
    It was not (yes, you thought it)
    From a girl that he caught it,
But from trying to read Browning's "Luria."

II

There was a young scholar of Spy Hill
Who retired after lunch to a high hill.
    Said his friends "Well, how was it?
    A healthy deposit?"
He sighed "Vox, et praeterea nihil."

III

There was a young man of Cape Town,
Who acquired European renown
    By sucking his come
    From his bugger-boy's bum,
Swallowing it, and keeping it down.

IV

There once was a Kensington Strumpet
Whose arse-hole would bray like a trumpet:
    Besides which gift, she
    Had one art, repartee.
As tasty and crisp as a crumpet.

So when her pa proved "a mere scum-pit
Your cunt is, and as for your rump, it
    Is all out of tune!"
    She laughed "yer baboon!
Yer don't like it? All right! yer can lump it!"

V

There was a young lady named Rose
Who filled not one po, but twelve poes
    With piss, sweat, and come,
    Thick slime from her bum,
And snot from her bloody old nose.

VI

There was an American whore
Whose cunt was a festering sore.
    She caulked it with pitch
    Till the bloody old bitch
Was A1 at Lloyds' evermore.

But with earthly success not content,
She grew pious — to Heaven she went.
    Son, Father, and Ghost
    And the heavenly host
Have all got the double event.

LIMERICKS

ADVENT

God is coming in the air;
Mary's cunt is on his face.
With her hands she frigs apace;
All the angels stand and stare.

Jesus sniggers "Ah, mon père!"
Cherubs whisper "See them race!"
God is coming in the air;
Mary's cunt is on his face.

Now the Ghost is in despair.
Did he pity Joseph's case?
Now a perfume fills the place,
And the heavenly host declare

"God is coming in the air."

THE SAILOR ASHORE

Give me a succulent twat!
Arsehole I'm weary of, straight!
Captain and bosun and mate,
Christ! I'm fair sick of the lot.

Slime, and shit in the slot!
What, would you make a bloke wait?
Give me a succulent twat!
Arsehole I'm weary of, straight!

Girls, are you pissing, or what?
I'm in a hell of a state!
Better than never is late!
Here is some spunk for you, hot.
Give me a succulent twat!

TRIOLETS

I shall write a short poem on cunt,
Explaining its delicate beauty;
Its folds, and its fronds, and its button.
Its scent, as of freshly killed mutton.
My language may seem very blunt;
But that is my fate, and my duty.
I shall write a short poem on cunt.
Explaining its delicate beauty.

The use of a cunt is to spend in;
The aim of a cunt is to spend.
Its neighbour the arsehole laments
That the folly of Nature prevents
It's helping the latter, to end in
Emission the gentleman's end.
The use of a cunt is to spend in;
The aim of a cunt is to spend.

Some people, avoiding the coarse word,
Describe it in roundabout fashion
As quim, or as cat, or as spot,
Or as oyster, or even as twat.
But I call turd, turd (it's a Norse word);
So cunt figures cunt to my passion.
Some people, avoiding the coarse word.
Describe it in roundabout fashion.

The clergy are partial to choir-boys;
I cannot approve of the taste.
For I prefer feeling or fucking
With occasional half-hours of sucking.
I think it is monstrous to hire boys
And pound up their shit into paste.
The clergy are partial to choir-boys;
I cannot approve of the taste.

The wonderful beauty of cunt
Is a thing for a poet to rave over!
At the moment of coming its grand;
They grip you and shake like a hand.
They emit a low poop, like a grunt;
And the jelly boils, flows like a wave over!
The wonderful beauty of cunt
Is a thing for a poet to rave over!

BIRTHDAY ODE

(To Percy Bowles Esq.)

There was a young bugger named Percy
Who let a most poisonous fart;
He collected the spend of an intimate friend
From the cunt of a two-penny tart.
This notorious whore had a tertiary sore
Halfway from her bubs to her belly;
He licked up the pus and distilled it for us!
With the toe-jam of M...e C.....i.

To continue his plan he looked up a man,
A fellow, who kept in the Cl.st.rs;
Who sucked off a pig (a magnificent frig)
Chewed that, and gave Percy the oysters.
Clap-juice he extracted from someone who acted
In the F..tl...ts (his acting was grand)
Then he sucked out the faeces and faeculent greases
From 45 whores in the Strand.

Still more to complete us he swallowed a foetus
Stewed whole with spew, monthlies, and snot.
The sauce was sublime; it was based on the slime
Of a fishwoman's rotten old twat.
He proceeded to suck the shit that had stuck
To the hairs on a bugger-boy's bottom.
Gulped down a placenta: drank piss and Apenta,
And said "Now I think chat has got 'em!"

He reserved every shot till the dinner was hot
And the people of "Sept" were content.
Then he fired off a whiff: Fat Bill gave a sniff:
"There's a curious sort of a scent!"
Alas for Fat Bill! Such a nosegay may kill!
Those words were the last that he uttered;

While Bowles gave a laugh like a cunt-stricken calf:
"Will you have them with Bovril, or buttered?"
Alas! The luck's ill! The house smashed like Fat Bill,
And went arse over tip like a lamp;
While the rest of us asked:— "Are our brains
    over-tasked?
There's an odour here! Can it be damp?"
Our souls went with Bowles to the heavenly goals
But we asked at the end of the tunnel:—
"Is this No. Seven? Or can it be heaven?"

He said:— "I am God and not Stannl."
We begged the Lord's pardon — walked round in
    his garden:
"This bower don't smell nice; I'll destroy it."
"The mistake's on Thy part! It's only my fart!
I hope J. and the Ghost will enjoy it."

ROSA MYSTICA

Rose, that you are a little sod
    Your shapely pouting arsehole shows.
Your tiny turds drop out like cod-Roes

From this our skepticism grows,
    And we may doubt the story odd
About the Ghost who gaily goes

(The priests say) to put you in a pod
    Your Jesus would not have a nose!
Your cunt would pox the eternal God, Rose!

T.J.

Toe-jam that oozes from thy feet,
　　Kate, I confess I am
Fond of, well fried in snot or gleet,
　　Toe-jam.

Better than buttered eggs, or ham;
　　Better than beef, or any meat!
Better than oyster, prawn, or clam!

Spread, spread the feast, disdainful sweet!
　　Call me to thee by telegram!
Take off thy socks and bid me eat
　　Toe-jam.

"SPLITS"

Who has not seen and envied (with a grunt)
The lusty partner of a maiden prance
Up and down gaily in a glorious country dance?

What joy have mariners to sail a brig!
Who knows not how they heed not, neither reck,
Or how a sailor loves a goodly frigate's deck?

Or his who leaves his wife, his only joy.
"Ah! Soul of mine, I weep that we must part."
Yet never goes abroad without a buoyant heart.

Such joys are his who loves the grassy knoll
And contemplates the sad, effusive me.
Nor seeks in vain the Virgin Mary's holy shrine.

CELIA

I

When Celia frigs my fat J.T.,
    Her mouth is luscious as a pig's:
I come three times in minutes three
    When Celia frigs.

But when she fucks, what randy jigs
    She dances on my stiff pee-wee!
I leave plain buggery to prigs!

Her twat is deeper than the sea;
    Her ulcers are like rotten figs;
— It is a holy time for me
    When Celia frigs.

II

When Celia spends I send a card
    Inviting all my oldest friends
To tea, if they can get a hard
    When Celia spends.

It should be easy to make ends
    Meet, O good comrades of the bard!
Her twat gapes wide: what Ghost descends

Upon that virgin hole? On guard!
    Brave soldiers. Frig ye! Fucking tends
To clap or chancre every yard
    When Celia spends.

III

When Celia farts, my hasty nose
    Sniffs up the fragrance of her parts.
Shamed are the violet and the rose
    When Celia farts.

From churning bowels the vapour starts;
    Through pox-gnawed cavities it blows:
Out at the anus worn it darts.

With rapture stiff my penis glows —
    Up, up her arse! Ye half-crown tarts,
I care no more to stuff your toes
    When Celia farts.

IV

When Celia pisses, I squat low
    Upon the floor for golden blisses.
White wine of love!
    My mouth the po.
When Celia pisses.

The silky stream is hot: it hisses
    Between the farts that mumble slow
Out of the sticky bum. God misses

A lot of fun. He doth not know
    How urine lubricateth kisses.
My cock doth stand: my spunk doth flow
    When Celia pisses.

V

When Celia fucks, my giant tool
   Goes in and out with mighty clucks:
My work's cut out, sir, as a rule
   When Celia fucks.

Worn by prolonged attempts on ducks,
   Weary of goats and boys, I school
With rods the unwilling slave: it plucks

Up heart for one more snooker's pool;
   It dives amid the mingled mucks
Of clap juice, come, and raspberry fool!
   When Celia fucks.

VI

When Celia comes, 'tis earthquakes hour!
   The bed vibrates like kettle-drums.
It is a grand display of power
   When Celia comes.

Right up her arse my shitty thumbs
   Increase her rapture. Gentle flower!
Flap go apace our bulging turns.

The sea hath swallowed up the tower.
   Spunk trickles over both our bums
In one ecstatic summer shower
   When Celia comes.

VII

When Celia's sick I shit my drawers,
　　Then wipe it up with them, then stick
My head therein. The poet scores
　　When Celia's sick!

The chunks I chew; the slime so slick
　　I mix with monthly blood — some whore's,
And oil with that my chancred prick.

We then start fucking on all fours.
　　Nine times, like Tite, I do the trick.
You bet the semen simply pours
　　When Celia's sick!

VIII

When Celia shits I bite my lips;
　　My cock gets fits;
I hold her hips
　　When Celia shits.

Chew, chew the bits!
　　The slime out slips
From stinking pits.

Her arsehole grips
　　My prick: my wits
Are in eclipse
　　When Celia shits.

IX

When Celia croaks I mean to play
    One of my funny little jokes,
Ah! Dust to dust and clay to clay
    When Celia croaks.

I'll dress her up in cloaks and toques
    Etcetera, earn her away
And after sundry final pokes

Hire her at three-and-six a day
    To G... H... — what a hoax!
"None but the dead" shall have its way
    When Celia croaks.

X

When Celia rots, each poxy hole
    Will serve: she hath an hundred twats.
Come finger, tongue, and fucking pole
    When Celia rots.

Here, the old ulcers! Happy spots!
    Hail, pustules! Hail, oh central goal
Wherein some sucking devil squats

Now surely as ever! Broke the bowl.
    Loosed the old cord — yet hope unblots
The record. God may fuck her soul
    When Celia rots.

SONG

Bugger me gently. Bertie! My arse is rather sore:
Tinkety — tunkety — tinkety — funk! I haven't been
    long a whore.
Mash the shit into gravy! Make me slimy and
    slick!
Tinkety — tunkety — tinkety — tunkety! That s what
    does the trick.

Bugger me gently, Bertie! My arse is rather tight.
Tinkers — tunkety — tinkety — tunk! We'll ram each
    other all night!
Bugger me gently, Bertie or I'll blow off your balls
    with a fart!
Tinkety — tunkety — tinkety — tunkety! Softly now,
    dear heart!

O Bertie, I'm in heaven! I see the golden walls!
Tinkety — tunkety — tinkety — tunkety! Shove it up
    to the balls!
Jesus is waiting for me with the Holy Ghost up his
    bum:
Tinkety — tunkety — tinkety — tunk! You bloody sod,
    you've come!

SONG

Buggered by a black man,
    Buggered by a Jew,
Buggered by a gentleman
    In navy blue.

The first costs a dollar,
    The second costs a quid,
The third costs you nothing,
    But you have to keep the kid

One kid's all right.
    Twins is a fraud,
Triplets split yer arse,
    Yer bet yer bloody Gawd!

One Gawd's Deism;
    Two's Manichee;
We're bloody Prodestunts,
    We run three.

Some's 'appy Cawthlics:
    Cuckolds an' 'ores
They like: in consikence
    Five they adores.

All little buggers
    What's gawt any sense
'Itches on a dildo,
    And damns the expense.

EPIGRAM

It's perfectly true though it sounds rather steep,
That a ram can satisfy 80 sheep.
Even so, I have doubts (though you tell me it's true)
If an 80 ram-man could satisfy you.

THE AUTOMATIC GIRL

I

The march of science in the land now marks an-
    other stride:
Not all in vain was Darwin's pain, that Bruno lived
    and died.
From Newton's toil we gain the oil to ease men's
    woes that whirl.
We now produce for public use the Automatic Girl.

II

She's warmed by electricity; she wags her arse by
    steam,
Her eye displays Marconi rays, a chemist makes
    her cream.
An antiseptic pussy-cat assures suspicious churls
That Jonathan has guaranteed our Automatic
    Girls.

III

Besides these marks of progress there's another
    gain to reap.
French girls are dear and Dutch, I fear, are dirty, if
    they're cheap.
We cater for the wants of all — a humble brown
    may twirl
Its easy passage through the slot of the Automatic
    Girl.

IV

The minor bard who got a hard was often forced to
  be
Familiar friends with odds and ends from Street to
  A.B.C.
But now at once the merest dunce may pluck the
  purest pearl.
By just — his pennies in the slot of the Automatic
  Girl.

V

Ye clerks, who get a sudden rise, be chary of your
  cash!
Society's and Beauty's eyes say "Cut a deadly
  dash!"
O no! Avoid Miss Marie Lloyd, the dunce's giddy
  whirl,
But put your pennies in the slot of the Automatic
  Girl!

VI

Ye cabmen wights so late o'nights that get upon
  the stand,
O let alone the reins you own! Refrain the shame-
  ful hand!
This fare you get you'll not regret, she will not
  make you curl!
So put your pennies in the slot of the Automatic-
  Girl.

VII

The young and old, the rich and poor, with us are
    well content.
[We take the stuff when there's enough and traffic-
    in cement.]
The son of dook, the son of cook, the son of belted
    earl
All put their pennies in the slot of the Automatic
    Girl.

CHORUS

And she'll work, work, work!
She'll give a nod
And say "My God!"
With a simper and a smirk.

She'll titillate your testes till with senses in a whirl
You plunge your pennies in the slot of the Auto-
    matic Girl.

GIRLS TOGETHER!

Piddling Polly and Randy Rose
Were maidens pure as Alpine snows.

Said Randy Rose to Piddling Polly:
How shall we cure this melancholy?

Said Piddling Polly to Randy Rose:
Let's put our hands up each other's cloches!

So Randy Rose and Piddling Polly
Frigged each other till they felt jolly.

Said Piddling Polly to Randy Rose:
There might be a prick downstairs — who knows?

Said Randy Rose to Piddling Polly:
A finger is fun — a fuck is folly.

Said Piddling Polly to Randy Rose:
I'm on for it anyway — here goes.

So Piddling Poll fetched a boy with a cock;
And was fucked for an hour and a half by the clock.

While Randy Rose sat over her head
And was sucked off seventeen times instead.

MICTURATING MARY

The well-bred wife of a high-church parson
    Had a daughter fair and merry
Who kept twelve hours a day her arse on
    The fine old family jerry.
She poured such a stream of waters vital
    From a cunt so slimy and hairy
That the Bishop of London gave her the title
    Of Micturating Mary.

One day they were praying in church for rain
    When the heavens above with a roar rent:
Came sizzle and splash on the window pane,
    And the road swirled down with the torrent.
Cried the vicar: "How quickly it's come to pass!
    Let's thank the Lord for his blessing!"
But his wife whispered "Hush! You silly old ass!
    It's only our Mary — confessing!"

Her father's curate entered her room
    With the fixed intention of fucking her;
But she went Pss-boom-whz-brr-pss-boom
    In spite of the corks she had stuck in her.
With her virgin cunt he lustily grapples,
    For she saucily, randily beckoned;
But she had to let go, and his rotten apples
    Were washed away in a second.

She angrily wired for Sir Walter Blunt
    "Come; bring down your scalpel and skewer,
And give me cunt that is cunt
    For a cunt that is only a sewer!"
So he chivied a hole from her bubs to her bladder
    And took out his penis and blocked her:
And thus the very first man that had her
    Was the eminent London Doctor.

She had triplets soon by the boy in the stable:
  There was Copulating Cora
And beautiful Mensurating Mabel
  And Defecating Dora.
Of all they did to tell you the story
  I may one day not be chary
For it all redounds to the honour and glory
  Of Micturating Mary.

But the Bishop ruined the Vicar's daughter.
  Though he usually kept it hidden, he
Had a tool in length a yard and a quarter.
  And it jiggered a hole in her kidney.
Her beautiful golden urine turned
  To a mucus ropy and glairy
And the meaning of "pains in the back" was learned
  By Micturating Mary.

The doctors did all they could to save her.
  She throve on a diet ascetic.
Till some silly ignorant bugger gave her
  Some gin as a diuretic.
For fifteen years without cessation
  Did the hissing torrents roll out;
And at the P.M examination
  They found she had pissed her soul out.

They carved a beautiful chamber-pot
  On her tomb: and this moral appear did:
"This elegant girl in an hour from her twat
  Poured more than the Nile in a year did.
Through the ages of earth her faultless fame
  Will never alter nor vary:
Stranger, hats off to the honoured name
  Of Micturating Mary!"

THE POET ABROAD

At Grindelwald I have no luck.
I want your pussy-cat to suck,
Your sniffy bottom-hole to fuck,
    My darling!

Remembrance is so sad for me!
I yearn for your K.U.N.T.
That in my mouth was wont to pee,
    My darling!

All on my balls you used to piss;
Your farts would smoke, your turds would hiss;
Then you would take my cock to kiss,
    My darling!

I used to hang on every word
Your dainty little mouth averred,
And make milk puddings with a turd,
    My darling!

I shat of yore between your bubs.
Those fat amusing butter-tubs:
Love's butterflies can grow from grubs,
    My darling!

Aye! 'Tis a keen remorseful knife
To think of you, my fucksome wife,
In this my solitary life.
    My darling!

It gives me very little pleasure
To dole out spunk by weight or measure
To any other lady's treasure,
    My darling!

The wall hath holes — I do not woo them.
The pillow creases — Je m'en fous them.
The sofa cracks — I spunk not through them,
    My darling!

Italian boys have bulging bums;
Their well trained arsehole fairly hums.
They shall not get my greasy comes,
    My darling!

My hand forgets its ancient cunning.
Before I knew you it was stunning:
I could toss off some twelve times running.
    My darling!

Now I am guiltless of a stand.
Only thy arse, thy twat, thy hand,
Thy lips could rouse me; that were grand,
    My darling!

I cannot piss: I cannot shite.
Come quickly to me, warm and white!
We'll fuck like buggery all night,
    My darling!

Aye! In your scented arms I'll creep.
We'll grip and kiss: we'll laugh and weep.
And fuck each other off to sleep,
　　My darling!

And after, when I come to die,
You'll lift your hot lascivious thigh
And squirt your spendings in my eye,
　　My Darling!

Then with your well worn chamois leather
You'll suck up, in your love's strong tether,
My last breath and last fuck together,
　　My Darling!

BIRCHGROVE PRESS
Flagellant & Libertine Erotica

———

Birchgrove Press specializes in producing new print and e-book editions of pre-1950s writings on sexual flagellation in English. Original editions of many of the books that we offer are difficult to obtain and are highly sought after. We are especially proud to offer new editions of rare Victorian flagellant texts such as *The Mysteries of Verbena House*, *Experimental Lecture by Colonel Spanker*, and *The Quintessence of Birch Discipline*. Birchgrove Press also produces new editions of libertine literature. We have published *Venus in the Cloister*, *The School of Venus*, *The Dialogues of Luisa Sigea*, and Isidore Liseux's translation of the Marquis de Sade's *Justine* (1791), *Opus Sadicum*, for example.

www.birchgrovepress.com.

www.ingramcontent.com/pod-product-compliance
Lightning Source LLC
Chambersburg PA
CBHW060124260626
47160CB00005B/2010